REX MUNDI

REX MUNDI

by

GEORGE SIMS

LONDON
VICTOR GOLLANCZ LTD
1978

© George Sims 1978

ISBN 0 575 02478 X

MADE AND PRINTED IN GREAT BRITAIN BY
THE GARDEN CITY PRESS LIMITED
LETCHWORTH, HERTFORDSHIRE
SG6 1JS

Olivier le Vasseur was one of the great pirates. Caught and sentenced to death, he flung a batch of papers at the crowd surrounding his scaffold with the cry,
"Find my treasure who can!"

REX MUNDI

1

THEO'S TAVERNA, Nissaki, Corfu.

These walls are, as they say, paper-thin. A fact I find continually irritating and inhibiting. If, by some fantastic stroke of luck, I was able to persuade Miss Nubile to visit my cubicle-like room I should not have the nerve to do more than hold her hand and whisper compliments.

Inhibitions concerning being heard at private matters plainly do not apply to some of Theo's customers. At night the sounds of creaking beds, incoherent snatches of conversation and bursts of laughter bring me back from the world of dreams, make me hold my breath and strain to make sense of what I hear, turning my head from side to side as if it were some kind of shoddy transistor radio which only operated when pointed straight at the broadcasting station. Never before have I spent so much time eavesdropping.

Last night I heard a husky female voice calling out blatantly, "Just there. Oh my God, that's it! S'right." Something a little theatrical about it to my ears which are sensitive to deception; years of being lied to by members of the British public have sharpened my reactions and, like some veteran hotel receptionist, I am always on the alert for anything that does not ring true. This nocturnal outburst sounded to me like a practised piece from a woman who has read too many magazine articles titled "Your right to an orgasm", etcetera. It woke me from a humiliating dream in which I had been an actor who forgot his lines just as the curtain was raised, and then I lay wide awake for an hour or more puzzled by the identity of the female concerned. Not Miss Nubile I think, as she would be unlikely to express herself in English at such a moment.

Odd, irrepressible desire to make these notes though I have no idea whether they are to form a record of a pleasant holiday, reaching its peak with Miss Nubile, alias Hildegarde Wegel, or to provide a basis for suing the travel company which put together this particular package deal. It is the first time that I have begun a journal. Usually I have an antipathy to putting pen to paper which prevents me from even entering my collar size or blood group in the diary which Aunt Margaret always gives me at Christmas.

Even stranger than this desire to write was the premonition of it which must have led me to buy the note-book. I entered the old-fashioned stationers in Lombard Street just for some blotting-paper, but once in there I found myself looking round with pleasure, largely because it was an unusual experience to be in a shop not filled with expensive rubbish. Like being in an ironmonger's or a saddler's shop, where most of the things appear to be well-made, useful and worth the money. This small octavo book, bound in serviceable blue cloth, with speckled edges, suddenly appeared very desirable.

I have been sidetracked from thinking about who could own that histrionic voice. It was sexy, but in a curiously unappealing, even repellent way. The sort of thing that makes one wonder whether premature impotence could be setting in, like an early frost, so that one is doubly grateful when Fraulein Wegel performs her graceful acrobatics on the beach.

Can I narrow down the possibilities regarding the mysterious voice by a process of elimination? No answer was the stern reply. So, here, a list of guests at Theo's Taverna, Nissaki, as of the 18th September 1976:

First floor

1st room : Dave Haswell and Ken Reardon. Two tough young Cockneys, both muscular and with the air of being professional athletes, expert swimmers and divers. Close friends tending to keep to themselves, even at times seeming more like conspirators than tourists, but not queer I should say, and certainly not female impersonators. No.

2nd room : Yours truly, H. J. Gilmour, sometime National Service private in the Gloucester Regiment, now a dealer in old and rare books whose only claim to fame is the smallness of his shop premises at Lilliput House, Mason's Yard, Duke Street, London, S.W.1. Harry Gilmour, aged forty-six but sometimes feeling older, who was wont to live with his wife Dorothy at Mulberry Cottage, Wardour, near Salisbury, but is now drifting away from her as she drifts away from him. Dorothy has sometimes accused me of muttering in my sleep, of "vague grumbling noises". I am willing to plead guilty to that charge as frustrations no doubt seek an outlet, but I'm certain I have never called out, "Just there. Oh my God. . . ." No.

3rd room : Hildegarde Wegel. German student. About the same age as my daughter Judith. With similar coltish movements and gaiety. A particularly fetching combination of long blonde hair, white teeth, delightful curves and broken English. The gods, with their unfailing sense of irony, placed her room next to the communal W.C. on this floor, so that I sometimes sit in there trying to ascertain whether she is next door and anxious not to make any lavatorial noises. This is the kind of hazard never mentioned in holiday brochures. And that's how constipation was born. Just possibly a candidate for that sexy voice but unlikely and I hope not.

4th room : Mr and Mrs Henry Merchant (from Canton, Ohio, U.S.A.). American tourists who seem to be finding it particularly difficult to adjust to the austere living conditions in Theo's Taverna. He is pleasant and friendly, but long-winded. She seems pleasant but is silent. Yes, Mrs Merchant may be a candidate for that voice though it does not seem to match up with her thin face and worried eyes. Yes and no.

5th room : Andrew Foster. Mr Average Man in appearance and difficult to describe. Mid-fifties, a widower he told me over a shared bottle of retsina. Possibly ex-R.A.F. He uses some of their dated slang. Exceptionally good eyesight, with a habit of commenting on small objects at great distances; the first time he did this I thought he was pulling my leg. Another habit of saying, "I thought you chaps would want to know" when bringing rumours of possible water shortages, deferred meals, cancelled expeditions, and so on. No.

Second Floor

1st room : Miss Jane Mackmurdo. Another attractive girl. Indefinable air of being "top drawer" and slightly out of her class on a package tour holiday; still, if it is good enough for a General it should be good enough for the Mackmurdo clan. She arrived with a perfect pale tan which has not been altered at all by exposure to the Corfu sun. Slightly prim, wary look but a mouth that turns up at the corners and reminds me of the Merry-mouth Inn. Sometimes has the manner of a precocious child. I was amused to see her sharing a table with Andrew Foster one evening and noted her attitude to him, charming but alert for the slightest sign of senility. Like Judith would be with me. Chekhov's saying about "daughters being like sparrows—they can't be deceived with chaff". Unlikely.

2nd room : Vacant. Shutters closed. I should have said the embarrassing outburst came from directly overhead, therefore from this room, but that does not make sense.

3rd room : Mrs Marianne Prothero. Fat woman with very white skin and abundant dark red hair. She has been a recluse since the first day here when she overdid the sun, wine and food. I thought she was in for trouble when her shoulders turned a shocking pink and she ordered a second bottle of wine and a dish of octopus as well as the red mullet and lamb kebabs. She was carrying a bottle of milk of magnesia and belching the only time I spotted her in the taverna. Any subsequent meals have been consumed in her room. Unlikely.

4th room: Claude Montefiore. French/Italian? Ugly swarthy man with lobster eyes. Fortyish. Each day nattily dressed in a different coloured light-weight suit, always looking cool and thoughtful. Away from Nissaki most of the time, driving a grey Citroën. Dines à la carte at a later hour than the rest of us. On very chummy terms with Theo. Most unlikely.

5th room: General William and Mrs Elizabeth Findlay-Duncan. The General is one of those rare, super-masculine characters with a mouth full of very small teeth. Also a disturbing habit of occasionally lifting his prognathous jaw in an expression of a will to win at any cost. Mrs Findlay-Duncan, usually quiet and subdued. The General always issues his orders to his wife; she passes them on in an aggrieved, slightly shrill voice. I once noticed her looking rather fuddled, mechanically thumbing through a book backwards. Unlikely.

I have scrutinised the list of Theo's guests twice and am no nearer to a decision about the voice. I have the inquisitiveness of the born detective but probably lack the necessary perception.

Pangs of hunger and the knowledge that we must wait for another half hour before the preliminary skirmishings of dinner commence with plates of olives and canned *bouzouki* music have led me to lose interest in the identity of the mystery woman and to re-read the misleading holiday brochure that brought me here. Having done so I am convinced that the firm gave the matter a good deal of thought and skilfully over-sold this place in terms with which one could argue but not litigate. I quote from page 12 of Corcyra Holiday Tours Brochure:

Theo's Taverna, Nissaki. Formerly a fisherman's house

poised on white rocks above a tiny harbour. Here you will dine under a velvet sky while watching the carbide lamps of fishing boats mirrored in the wine-dark Ionian Sea. Ask for *Kephtaydes* (highly spiced meat balls), *Pattischada* (macaroni pie), *Melitzanes* (fried egg-plant) or *Souvlakhia* (delicious spitted meat). . . .

All masterly stuff. I'm sure that if you were to complain to the tour firm about the uncertain water-supply, the doll-sized hand-basin and wardrobe, the matchboard partition that separates the W.C. from Hildegarde Wegel's room, they would reply that such things are inevitable if you are going to live in what was formerly a fisherman's cottage. And it is true that one could ask Theo for any of the dishes they list, or for Beluga caviare for that matter, but all he would have on offer would be olives, the ubiquitous goat cheese salad, red mullet, lamb kebabs, and the dreaded *Ochtapodi* which apparently did for Mrs Marianne Prothero.

Still, it is true that most of the day here passes agreeably. The swimming and skin-diving are excellent. The beach is pleasant though small. One can try sailing in a caique, something Haswell and Reardon do very well but I shall never master. And a speed-boat calls in at the tiny harbour regularly twice a day for those who want to do water-skiing. I managed to get up first time simply by lying back in the sea and not caring whether I made a fool of myself, saying, "Here I go, down the drain", and making a mental inventory of all that Dorothy would inherit if I fell under the propeller. I decided I was worth more dead than alive and made an extremely cautious circuit, like an invalid, only to find on my return to the beach that my feeble performance had been taking place under the steady, mocking gaze of Miss Jane Mackmurdo and General Findlay-Duncan.

Nevertheless, from breakfast till say 7 p.m. it is pleasant enough to be staying at Theo's Taverna. It is during the next hour or so, when the sun has gone down over the other side of the mountain and a freshening breeze blows in from the sea, that one gets tired of sitting by the quay and is forced to return to these tiny, inadequate bedrooms.

The welcome sound of *bouzouki* music below. This means that if Theo can be persuaded to curtail his Zorba the Greek dancing among broken tumblers, we may soon be eating our red mullet.

Postscript. Popped back just to record a vignette. Went up to the W.C. on the second floor in order to have an uninhibited pee and passed Mrs Prothero's room. The door was open and she was seated on the bed, with a disconsolate expression, sorting through bottles of pills and medicine.

2

"Idiot." Lying on the beach with my face pressed down into a towel, this provocative word woke me from a dream in which I had been a different kind of man, light-hearted and more likeable. I returned reluctantly and with difficulty; I had been drugged by an over-long swim. I sighed into my towel, lifted my head with what seemed an extraordinary amount of effort and looked up to see Andrew Foster staring down at me with a puzzled, worried expression.

"Oh, sorry, so sorry, old man. I didn't realise you were having a nap. I was just saying about this unpleasant encounter with a very odd bod. A giant. . . ."

Having returned from the strange world of dreams, it seemed important to restrain flights of fancy. "Really? A giant?"

"Well, abnormally tall then. 'Bout six six. Very pale blond hair and those kind of eyebrows so fair you can hardly see 'em. Gave me a *very* funny look. He was standing in the shade of an olive tree on the road up there. . . ."

"Perhaps a Scandinavian? Just arrived this morning and overwhelmed with the heat," I suggested.

"No, that was a very funny look he gave me, old man. As though he was trying to memorise my appearance. Thought he might be some kind of village idiot, but he wasn't dressed for the part. Wearing a smart grey suit. I couldn't help looking back and by God there he was, still at it."

I shrugged. I couldn't work up much interest in the sinister blond giant. Foster stood on tiptoe to survey the narrow road winding down to the harbour. "Think he's gone now. Good riddance. Shouldn't want to bump into him again today. By the way, I think you should know, I should steer clear of the rocks the other side of the jetty."

"Why's that? It's not a dangerous spot. Crystal clear there. You can see each rock when you dive. . . ."

"No, not that. I saw Theo and Evstratios killing a great brute of an eel there. It had a head like a dog and a rat-trap mouth. They were hacking away with an axe and a fork to kill it. Then bundled it off in a sack, and kept very quiet about it."

"Yes, well, that's certainly something to bear in mind."

"I say, see the General going off to town."

I stood up, shook out my towel and watched General Findlay-Duncan getting into his tiny, hired car with a straw shopping basket.

Foster smiled faintly. "There he goes, off to market like little Red Riding Hood and woe betide any wolf that gets in his way."

"Amen to that." I rearranged my towel even closer to the sea's edge hoping that the lulling waves might induce another pleasant dream, and Foster moved off saying, "Well, see you later then, Harry. A drink before lunch?"

"Fine. That will be nice."

Foster paused again, waving his hand vaguely at the horizon, and I thought he might be going to comment on some bird that had alighted on the distant Albanian shore, but he merely said, "Very beautiful here, old man."

I looked out over the mirror-like vista contrived by sunshine, sea and sky, saying, "Yes, it quite makes up for all that Greek dancing."

Foster walked along the beach past Reardon and Haswell who were dragging a caique out of the sea. Lying down again, I watched big ants struggling over stones with carcases of beetles larger than themselves and thought about William Findlay-Duncan, the first British General I had ever seen at close quarters despite my two years in the army and six months active service in Korea. I had overheard some of his *sotto voce* comments to his wife and they had all been in a similar biting vein, "As rich as wedding-cake", "What an extraordinary young woman", "Lurking in doorways again". I had also heard him deliver an authoritative sentence to Henry Merchant in the bar: "A man who says he is not afraid to die is a liar and more afraid than one who admits his fear."

"Oh, Mr Gilmour." I turned and found that the owner of the agreeable girlish voice was Mrs Prothero. She and Jane Mackmurdo were descending the beach in my direction in a purposeful way. Marianne Prothero was protected from the sun by an attractive filmy silk garment which reached practically to her ankles, and she seemed quite recovered from her various ills. She smiled at me and her manner was decidedly skittish. Miss Mackmurdo's attitude was neutral, like an observer at a ceremony. She wore a white cotton shirt over brief denim shorts, and a small white cotton hat. She carried her smoke-blue sun glasses so they did not put their usual barrier between us.

Mrs Prothero shook her finger at me. Her manner hovered on the edge of being flirtatious. "Now I've got you. Well, I think so at least. Do you know, your name and face have been worrying me ever since our first day here."

I never know how to handle personal remarks. My first reaction was to make a facetious apology for any trouble my face had caused, then I thought no, play it cool like Miss Mackmurdo would. So I simply said, "Really?"

"Yes. Very much so. I have this kind of photographic memory but a bad filing system, if you know what I mean. I knew it struck a vague chord. . . . Anyway, I think I have it now. You were in the papers recently! Wasn't it some kind of funny headline?"

"I expect the reporter thought it might raise a grin. Surprised you should remember it. I buy and sell old books. Went to an auction in London and bought a box of Russian pamphlets and newspapers—very cheaply. A reporter got to hear of it and wrote it up. An exaggerated version to give it more punch as a story."

"You're being coy about that headline."

"Not at all. 'Sold to the man from the doll's house shop.' There you are. You see, my shop is a very small one, called Lilliput House, just off Duke Street, in Mason's Yard." I enjoyed giving my address to Miss Mackmurdo in this off-hand way but she did not seem to be making a note of it. I could smell her faint seductive perfume. She was giving me a good look over as if I were a second-hand car. But thirty years of boxing and swimming have left me with a body that looks at its best in a swimming costume. I look at my worst in January, in an overcoat.

Miss Mackmurdo smiled in a rather delightful way and addressed her first sentence to me. "Must have been an exciting find for you. Do you specialise in Russian books?"

"Not only don't specialise, I don't know a single word of Russian and usually don't have a Russian book in stock. This lot just happened to belong to an old customer of mine, a Polish Jew who was born in Russia in the 1890s, moved to Poland in the '20s and England in 1937."

Mrs Prothero wagged her head doubtfully. Her eyes, lighter brown than those of Jane Mackmurdo, were used to probing; I could well imagine them concentrating on images for her mental stereopticon. "How come? That you bought the box so cheaply I mean. I thought that sort of bargain didn't happen nowadays at London auctions."

"Well, to start with it was a very small saleroom tucked away in Pimlico. And then, Dolek's possessions. . . . The old man was called Dolek Menkes. He had no relatives, and all his things were put into what they call an executor's sale. A very rough and ready affair. One wooden box full of Jewish religious paraphernalia. One wine-carton with the pamphlets shoved in anyhow and described in the list simply as 'Russian magazines, a box'. There were a few early Soviet leaflets among them, and the reporter seized on that. Made it all sound more interesting than it really was."

"What do you think they're worth?" Mrs Prothero's eyes shone at the thought of large amounts of cash.

"Not a fortune. I got a specialist to look at them. Perhaps fifteen hundred pounds."

"Is that all?"

"That's it. And due to that ridiculous press story we may be getting a rat-tat on the door at Lilliput House one day from some Soviet agent. . . ."

"Ah well," Mrs Prothero cut off my flight of fancy. "Nothing's perfect." Her eyes made it plain that any interest in me had been extracted; it was like the lowering of the film that passes over a parrot's eyes. She took hold of Jane Mackmurdo's arm possessively. "Look, there's the motorboat with that crazy Tracy girl. Shall we see if she's really fixed up that trip to Sidari?"

They left me feeling slightly like a squeezed lemon but, looking out at the bald profile of the Albanian coast, I experienced a more unpleasant sensation than deflation. Momentarily I felt as if I was drifting away from everything about me, like a spaceman falling in slow motion into unending space. Though it was a very hot day I shivered, with a premonition of a darkening future. Then I picked up my towel and hurried across to the quay. I needed a few slugs of retsina before Andrew Foster joined me.

3

Elizabeth Findlay-Duncan regarded the waiter's back with a resentful uneasiness, as if she did not like the set of his shoulders. She cleared her throat, moved her empty glass to the centre of the table with great care and said, "A little chilly now. Think I'll go in."

The General shifted in his chair, a perfunctory movement to indicate a willingness to rise, and I stood up. He nodded gravely, saying "All right, my dear. Shan't be long myself." Once again I had the feeling that there was no love lost between the two of them; that politeness was all.

Mrs Findlay-Duncan walked across the quay in the direction of the taverna with a tense, staggering gait, appearing quite befuddled by drink despite having consumed only one glass of white wine while at our table. She reminded me of an alcoholic I used to see in a pub in Duke Street, a woman with an enormous congested old face, always cradling in her arms a dribbling pekinese. She had the same air of determined concentration needed to make sense of anything said to her. Some serious drinking must go on behind the closed shutters of the General's room. They seemed to spend a good deal of time apart; he away from Nissaki most days, driving in his orange Renault, she sitting listlessly in a deckchair holding an unopened paperback.

The General clicked his third left finger on his thumb and his lips moved silently. His left leg stuck out awkwardly askew. Most of the time one would hardly be aware that he had a game leg. The only clues were an occasional difficulty in getting into his small car, and a momentary hesitation when rising from a chair. I had noticed how cleverly he dissembled the stiffness while climbing stairs.

In his dark blue silk shirt and silver-grey lightweight trousers, immaculately creased, the General looked a model of neatness. A meticulous man, always in control of himself, a man unlikely to waste time brooding on failures or be inflamed by memories of miscarried projects.

I had been puzzled when the General invited me to join him and his wife for "a glass of wine before dinner", but a few minutes of his adroit questioning led me to realise that he must have heard from Andrew Foster about my stint in Korea. His questions were nicely calculated to discover whether I had actually been in action at the front or a Stores Wallah in Pusan.

"So many foreigners out there. Canadians, Turks, Filipinos. God knows what. Any with you?" The General turned to regard me with cornflower blue eyes that had undoubtedly seen much service in questioning subordinates.

"I spotted General Yazici, the Turkish commander, once but there weren't any Turks with us. Twenty-nine Brigade was made up of Northumberland Fusiliers, Royal Ulster Rifles and the Gloucesters. And a Belgian battalion. Called 'The Old Man's Brigade' because it consisted largely of reservists in their thirties."

"But you wouldn't have been in your thirties then?"

"No, I had my twenty-first birthday out there. In Taegu. A squalid collection of mud huts and hovels on the Naktong River."

"Didn't you chaps . . . the Gloucesters . . . didn't you have a nick-name too?"

"Yes, the Gloomys. Because we were rather a quiet bunch."

"You were there for the big do? On the Imjin River? Some unpleasant memories I expect?" The General's tone was light, but he appeared to study my face with interest. It may have been because of the failing light, but I got the impression that he wanted some of those memories to compare with his own.

"Memories?" I pretended to give the matter thought

but plenty came to mind. Ice-hard in the packed snow, the Chinese soldiers had looked very young and delicate. I remembered one frozen corpse sitting bolt upright, bent like that by some trick of contraction induced by napalm. The Chinese didn't wear the padded khaki winter clothing of the North Koreans but merely three or four layers of thin cotton cloth. I had been through the pockets of one of them and found he was carrying only two ammunition clips, a bone seal for signing his name, and one of the "safe-conduct for prisoners" passes that our air forces had been dropping over the enemy lines. I thought the General would not believe me if I told him that my most abiding memory of Korea was that of the Siberian wind, an eerie wind that would blow for three days, lowering the temperature about fifteen degrees, but with a much greater effect on the human spirit, sapping morale and creating fear.

"Yes, we might take a hill in about a day if it was lightly defended. Then we would sit on top of it and just wait for 'the patter of tiny feet', the Chinese counter-attack at night. Always began with them blowing bugles and whistles. That first bugle call was as bad as anything. . . ."

"No retreat, no retreat. They must conquer or die who have no retreat." The General said this with a stagey gesture. It sounded like a well-practised piece. He opened his eyes very wide, giving some matter concentrated thought, then nodded vigorously as if assenting to a string of suggestions. "Yes, yes, yes. Very lucky to have survived all that and be sitting here in this beautiful spot." With a wave of his arm he indicated the outline of a misshapen fig-tree silhouetted against the sunset. "Interesting . . . Very interesting talking to you, Gilmour, but . . . Time to change now . . . Leave you to finish . . . Drink in peace. . . ." He got straight up by some trick of leverage and walked off without a hint of stiffness.

I looked round at the papery ilex-tree shivering in the freshening breeze, the pin-pricks of light from carbide lamps out at sea and the sun just disappearing over the rim of the mountain, and had to agree that at least the brochure had not over-sold the natural beauty of Nissaki. From the rapidly darkening beach I heard a stifled exclamation, and walked over to the rails at the edge of the jetty to see if Theo and Evstratios were battling with another giant eel. Instead I found that Haswell and Reardon were once again struggling with their small hired caique, having some difficulty in beaching it. They both looked exhausted.

Reardon sat down heavily once the boat was safe. "And I say give up."

Haswell regarded him in silence for a few moments, his barrel chest heaving. "Christ Almighty! Come all this bleedin' way, spend half a grand, then it's difficult so you say give up. For fuck's sake. . . ."

"All right. All right. Tonight I've 'ad it, tomorrow. . . ."

It was interesting stuff and I should have liked to learn more, but I was having to lean forward to pick up what they were saying and I realised that if one of them turned round I should be seen clearly to be spying on them. Eavesdropping was becoming a habit with me and I should have to cut it out, at least in public. I retreated silently.

4

KISSES SHOULD BE silent. This idea came to me like
a gift from nowhere and seems to be worth recording. At
first I thought of the precept in relation to the five or six
women with whom I am on kissing terms in public, with
Dorothy's approval as she in turn gets kissed by the hus-
bands. It is usually a rather silly event with smacking kisses
and exclamations of "M-m-m", as though they were
kissing an aged relative.

However, I think my subconscious may have prompted
this thought in protest at the extraordinary goings-on here
last night with loud kisses, a bed thumping away somewhere above me, and that preposterous throaty voice call-
out, "Oh yes, my lord and master, oh yes, that was truly
wonderful". Such behaviour is both absurd and embarrassing in these confined quarters. Like a nightmare in that
during the day it does not seem possible, for who of the
rather ordinary bunch staying here could get up to such
capers?

If I try to be honest, if I probe a little deeper, may
there not be a twinge of jealousy in my reaction to these
night-noises, to do with the knowledge that there would
be no such sounds from our room if Dorothy was staying
here with me? A graph of the relationship of some couples
would be like the temperature chart of a feverish patient,
fluctuating continually and reaching peaks of crisis; that of
our marriage would more resemble a firm going bankrupt,
with steadily diverging lines of overheads and profit. It is
typical that Dorothy has gone on holiday to Iceland while
I am in Corfu; that she likes walking tours and seeing places
of interest while I only want to swim and soak up the sun.

One of the troubles is that we have both reached the age when one no longer changes but becomes more oneself.

Break off these philosophical notes to record that I heard the magical phrase "and miss a fucking fortune" from the next door room shared by Haswell and Reardon. I immediately went over to the plasterboard partition and pressed my ear to it but the result was unsatisfactory, picking up only tantalising snatches of a conversation conducted in whispers despite the fact that they were quarrelling.

"A crock of gold."

"With a bit of luck."

"Don't like the look of that."

"We could do with dainty."

After the odd word "dainty" there was a short silence as if Fear and Suspicion had sneaked into that small room.

When the stage-whispered duet started again reception was worse, so that I made out only odd words: "Lump", "doubloons", "you", "off". The conversation was ended by a door being slammed, and then slammed again after a few seconds interval.

Intriguing. But can I have got those fragments right? Can there really be doubloons off the Corfu coast? Would a tough young Cockney really want or refer to something as dainty? Nevertheless treasure could certainly be an explanation of all that professional looking diving equipment, the coils of nylon rope, their secretiveness and dedication, the long hours they spend in the caique, their apparent lack of interest in any other pleasures offered around here.

Possibly my age has something to do with this strange desire to get my thoughts on paper for the first time in my life. Reaching forty-five now seems to me to have marked the end of a period when I was always sustained by the vague hope that something would come along to change my life without my doing anything in particular to bring it about. Now I know different. Unless I make a break soon my life will continue in a rut. I need to pull off a coup, to find "a fucking fortune" in fact. I want to live it up for a few years before the epoch of false teeth and arthritis sets in. Perhaps I should set out to demonstrate my diving prowess in front of Reardon and Haswell. I can hardly offer to help in whatever they are finding so difficult to accomplish but, by God, I'd like to.

That latest bit of eavesdropping left me restless and even more unlikely to get to sleep. What I was in the mood for was adventure. I thought of the possibility and my mind darted far ahead, sending back a signal about the difficulties of smuggling doubloons out of Corfu. And all this before I could even visualise the slightest chance of joining the treasure-hunt.

I paced the tiny room like a caged animal, picking up a crumpled shirt and then my own skin-diving gear which looked like a child's in comparison with the sophisticated equipment possessed by Reardon and Haswell.

I glanced at a coloured postcard from Dorothy chronicling her progress in Iceland: a rather stark view of "Krisuvik. The steam jet and mud cauldron". And on the other side:

Dear H. All well now that we have left Reykjavik. Pony trekking along rough tracks over moraines of black sand. Moss campion, saxifrage, thrift and dwarf willow; many of the alpine flora in fact. Letter from Judith who seems so pleased I am going on to Hamburg that I may stay longer there than planned. Hope you are enjoying Nissaki and getting plenty of swimming. Don't take any foolish risks diving. Hvitarvatn beautiful I thought but too much ice for your taste, close to Langjokull, the third largest ice-cap in the country. Forgot to bring my camera! What an idiot! Food dull. Send me a card. Love D.

I mused on the irony of Dorothy warning me against "diving", meaning my usual antics off rocks which are about ninety per cent danger free, while Haswell and

Reardon must actually be engaged in really dangerous underwater work.

Again the sound of music from above. There's another romantic penned up in one of these coops. The third time I have heard the waltz "Ohne mich" from *Der Rosenkavalier*. I tried to imagine who could have gone to the trouble of bringing a record-player in their weight-limited luggage. I decided to walk out on the narrow, communal balcony, a thing I had previously avoided in case Hildegarde Wegel should think I was intruding on her privacy.

I turned off my bedside lamp and stepped out into the soft night air, scented with herbs. I was greeted by a moon of unbelievable size; its light made a sequined path on the sea. Sounds of cicadas were mixed up with the German duet.

"Moonlight can be cruelly deceptive, Amanda." I said this quietly in my best Noël Coward voice but immediately heard someone above me laugh in response. Looking up I caught sight of Jane Mackmurdo's face, pale in the moonlight.

"So it's you who plays the Strauss and Chopin."

"Guilty. Not too late is it? I went for a super long walk. Haven't looked at my watch since."

"Not eleven yet. Besides, that's a favourite piece of mine. Quite fantastic in this setting."

Jane Mackmurdo looked down at me in silence and, under the magical influence of moonlight and *Der Rosenkavalier*, we both went on smiling. She leaned further forward and asked, "Shall you be going on the yacht to Sidari?"

"The trip being organised by Tracy? Do you think it might actually come off? None of her expeditions have materialised so far. That lobster dinner at Ipsos. . . ."

"The grottos at Paleokastritsa . . . The Kaiser's throne . . . No, I know, but this time it may be different. She's actually taken bookings for Sidari. Money has changed hands. Verily she hath my drachmas."

"In that case I'll say yes. I'd very much like to see the north coast of the island."

"Well, Tracy said tomorrow if it's fine. On a 'super green and white yacht' that belongs to some eccentric American! She's promised us a lobster lunch at Sidari too, but we'll see."

Jane smiled at me again and I was struck by the candour of her expression. It seemed that due to a shared enthusiasm for Richard Strauss and my Noël Coward quip we had slipped into an easy relationship. A tiny wave from her and my nod in response was our mute goodnight.

5

A s we turned Karagol Point the sea became clearer and yet more mysterious, disclosing its bed of white rocks festooned with sea-urchins, and flashes of silver fish among dark banks of weed. Movements fathoms deep invented mirages of shadow.

The yacht, unlike many of Tracy Jones' plans, had indeed materialised. It was named *Freedom*; all glossy peacock-green and white paint, with brass fittings and a white awning. It was not sailed by an eccentric American but by an old Greek called Niko and a boy. The old man had cropped, grizzled hair and a face burnt practically black by the sun; he wore black serge trousers and a homely woollen vest; he did not understand English and babbled away in Greek to Tracy who probably understood one word in two. The shabbily dressed, handsome boy did not speak at all but smiled a lot.

Thumbnail portrait of Tracy Jones, courier to Corcyra Holiday Tours, and temporary resident of Ipsos: a tall, raffish-looking girl, whose garish makeup appeared to have been applied without reference to a mirror; usually "just dashing off", always improvising and apologising; always carrying a Japanese Air Lines shoulder-bag bulging with passports, tickets and documents.

Tracy drove a loud, unreliable moped. She was fluent in French and *franglinika*, that odd combination of French, English and Greek. She adjusted her English vocabulary to clients of different ages, substituting "balls-up" or "cock-up" for "mess-up". She had a stock of phrases which could be applied to most situations: "What a lark!"; " 'Fraid I don't twig", "Mr Thing's fault", "Over the moon", "Virtually unobtainable", "I'm not into that yet", "It's all here, love, in lip-movers' print", the last when referring to her well-thumbed copy of the Corcyra Holiday Tours Brochure. She seemed to be stuck for words only when confronted by General William Findlay-Duncan.

Tracy had the look of failure written all over her, like one of those "emancipated" ageing models to be seen humping a large costume bag and chasing after a bus in London. I could not visualise her shaking down any of life's great prizes and so I had silently enlisted on her side.

As we sailed closer to the shore by the tiny harbour at Kouloura, Tracy was bending down and talking to Mrs Prothero who lay prone beneath the awning, with an additional small tent contrived from a towel to protect her sunburnt ankles. I heard Tracy calling on her usual authorities "Mr Thing" and "Mr What's-his-name", and Mrs Prothero's reply, "Don't try to promote a promoter, dahling."

The trip to Sidari had to be judged a success at the outset if only in the number of Theo's customers who had been attracted to it. It was no wonder that Theo himself had appeared to wave us off. Ten of his customers were going to be away for lunch, and Theo did not know the meaning of the word refund. Only the General and his wife remained at Nissaki.

As I took my place on the jetty Jane Mackmurdo had whispered conspiratorially, "All aboard for the mystery tour". I had been surprised to see that Mrs Prothero, the Merchants, Foster, Miss Nubile, Reardon, Haswell, and even Claude Montefiore were joining us. It was true that Montefiore had hesitated on the ladder, viewing the yacht "Freedom" with malevolent dark eyes as though he might change his mind, but once on board he had settled down with a Greek newspaper.

For the first half-hour of the trip Andrew Foster had talked to me solidly; an encapsulated account of his life since the age of twenty-two when he joined the R.A.F. He had flown for six months during the Battle of Britain with Fighter Command, then joined Trainer Command and spent three years in Canada. Subsequently he had worked at one of the City branches of Barclays Bank as a securities clerk. Inheriting "a tidy sum" from an aunt, he had retired early. A widower for four years, he lived by the Thames at Cookham Dean. He said his one luxury was a Cessna aircraft which he kept at Booker Airfield.

I enjoyed absorbing this information while I soaked up the sun. I only needed to nod and add the odd word from time to time as Foster seemed to be in the mood for autobiography. As Kouloura receded into the distance he stood up, unfolding his Fairey Corfu map and saying, "Nearest we shall ever get to Albania, old man". I stood up too and asked, "May I have a look at the map?" I wasn't stirred by our present proximity to Albania, but I had been suddenly struck by the absurd hope that there might be a little engraving of a galleon on the map showing where the Santa Maria or some such craft had sunk in 1572. My optimism was not justified. After I had murmured, "Ah yes, I see", Foster took out his binoculars from an old-fashioned leather case and moved round the deck to scrutinise the Albanian mountains.

Tracy had stopped promoting Mrs Prothero; she leaned against a bulwark, staring down at her scruffy plimsolls with a look of moody introspection. She wore bell-bottomed jeans and a white T-shirt with the word KILLER in black lettering across the chest. It seemed as if she might be brooding on her palpably doubtful future. She had told me of her vague plans for joining a French ski holiday firm as a courier at Christmas, but even if that came off there would be a gap when the Corfu season finished. Catching my glance she snapped out of her mood and came over to me.

"Well, what do you think, Harry? Isn't it great?"

"Fantastic. Didn't expect anything so millionaireish."

"I know. But you see this guy, Jake Thing, who owns it, well Niko looks after it all year round and Jake What-

• •

you-m'call-it, he's often away, so Niko has his okay for day charters like this. I mean, it's all on the up and up. Niko calls the boat a *'lordiko'*. Such wonderful craftsmanship that's what I like about it. Carvel built, you know. Means the planks meeting flush at the seams, instead of overlapping."

"And we seem to be really speeding along. Must be making very good time."

"Yes love, but we shall have to just pop in at Aghios Stephanos. Something Niko wants to collect there. Only for a quarter-of-an-hour though, and there's a tiny taverna. Very quaint and right off the tourist track. . . ."

Tracy walked off to jolly along the Merchants, who were sitting in silence. Mrs Merchant's face looked rather pale and she seemed to be holding herself rigid, as though any movement might be fatal.

I pretended to be taking in the beauties of nature but actually was studying the youthful group made up of Reardon, Haswell, Hildegarde and Jane at the rear of the yacht. Reardon and Haswell looked completely relaxed and as if they had forgotten the frustrations of treasure-hunting. Hildegarde wore an eye-catching bright green bikini, but I thought that Jane looked even more fetching in a yellow cotton blouse worn over white shorts with white sandals and the kind of yellow cotton hat with a brim that children used to wear on seaside holidays. Haswell was having some success in making the girls laugh. I had suspected he had a sense of humour when I walked past him once as he was doing press-ups on the beach and he had said, "That's enough. I don't want to get too strong."

Ah well, I thought, that's how it should be, they're all the same age-group. And anyway, can forty-six pursue twenty-two without making a fool of himself? Twenty-two is living a different kind of life, fresher, first-hand; forty-six's thoughts and feelings are tired and second-hand. This bit of pessimistic philosophy did the trick for while I was working it out Jane detached herself and came and sat

33

down beside me. Neither of us said anything immediately and this very silence was the sign of a different stage in our relationship. I sat back, staring up at the sails straining in the wind.

Jane leaned forward suddenly. "How's that for a house? M-m! I don't usually covet other people's possessions but I'll make just one exception...."

She was pointing at a superb house of white stone perched on the white rock headland at Aghios Stephanos. It was difficult to see where the cliff finished and the walls began; in places the walls were actually overhanging the sea.

For some reason, probably to do with underwater hazards, Niko was taking the yacht practically up to the cliffs before swinging it round and into the small bay. The white rocks took on an unreal sheen in the glaring sunlight.

"Yes," I said, "if the eccentric American millionaire who owns this yacht wanted to give me that house I could be persuaded."

"Not owned by an American. A White Russian Prince—been here ever since he escaped from the revolution. All the furniture's white, with white rugs everywhere. He's up in that room there, right at the top, playing a white Bechstein Grand...."

"Always wears white clothes too, with a white Panama hat," I suggested as Jane's imagination faltered. "Looked after by two devoted White Russian servants."

"They'd be rather old now for servants."

"He doesn't care about that. A very selfish old White Russian Prince. He chose this headland because it's the closest spot on the island to Russia. What a place!"

As if to demonstrate his ease in handling the yacht, Niko was taking *Freedom* in parallel and very close to the rocks. Rock thistle, cactus and mesembryanthemum grew at the bottom of the white cliffs. The rear of the white stone house was guarded by a group of cypresses and dusky purple Judas trees.

34

The grinning barefoot boy leapt on to a white sea-wall and tied up the yacht. The white rocks had the sheen of a bleached bone and the reflected sunlight was quite dazzling. Jane popped on her sun-glasses. "I'm shy," she explained. "Usually I use these to hide behind, but today I'm glad I've got them."

I looked down into the crystal clear water between us and the sea-wall. Minute fish were darting about over clean stones, green fragments of glass, sea charcoal and bladderwort. "Aghios Stephanos"—I said the name slowly as if it were a talisman—"Fantastic place! I think I'm going to remember it."

"You're right. We must be nice to Tracy. We've got something to be grateful for even if the sacred lobster doesn't materialise."

Niko produced a wooden ladder and he and the boy handed us safely on shore as though we were objects of great frailty. There was a hanging screen of olive branches on the white sea-wall. Bumble-bees made the only sound apart from quietly lapping water.

Tracy guided us along a path of white sand, encroached on by a huge fig-tree, to a point where it joined a track going right and left. She pointed left to a handful of small buildings. "The taverna's down there. It's great."

I glanced at my watch. "All right if I get back to the yacht in fifteen minutes? I don't want a drink. Okay? Feel like mooching around."

" 'Kay Harry." Tracy shook a finger at me. "But don't be late now." She grinned, probably assuming that I felt the need to pee in absolute privacy, rather than in the tiny toilet on the yacht.

I waited for a few moments as the rest of the group made their way down to the taverna and then walked off briskly in the other direction. Curiosity killed the cat, I thought, that would make the ideal epitaph for me. I wanted to have a closer look at the grand house that had been built in such a remote position. I walked up through a myrtle grove and past a clump of eucalyptus trees swarming with bees.

The track led to massive black iron gates set in a white stone wall some ten feet high. There appeared to have been successive attempts to make the smooth wall insurmountable. Small pieces of glass had been cemented on the top and they sparkled in the sun with glints of blue and red and green. Above this there was an arrangement of iron spikes similar to the one that guards the walls of Buckingham Palace. Barbed wire had been interwoven in this mediaeval barbarism.

I held the iron bars of the gate and peered through at the house which was half hidden by cypresses and Judas trees. It was of a simple Moorish design but superb proportions. An umbrella-pine grew so close that it tapped on the roof of terracotta tiles. Most of the shutters were in place but there were a few dark, inanimate windows. Above the persistent murmur of bees I could hear only the sound of a fountain. To the right of the house I saw a man in a sunlit clearing negligently flicking dust from a white Mercedes limousine with a yellow cloth.

There were two bolts on the iron gate, and a large unfastened padlock hung suspended on a thick chain. There was no need for a sign saying PRIVATE—KEEP OUT! Anyone who would go to the expense of having such a place built at the tip of a headland in a remote part of Corfu, and then surround it with a ten foot wall and barbed wire, must have an obsessive desire for privacy. The house was indeed a masterpiece of a kind but its atmosphere was mysterious, even faintly menacing.

W E   T R O O P E D   A S H O R E at Sidari, hot, hungry, and
pleased to be on land again. The trip from Aghios
Stephanos had taken longer than expected as the wind had
died down, leaving us becalmed in the Bay of Apraos.
Eventually Niko had despaired of a breeze, and from
Spiridon Point, past Cape Aghios, the long Roda Beach,
Cape Roda and Cape Astrakari we had chugged steadily
but slowly, powered by diesel.

Once the yacht was safely tied up at a small jetty, Niko
and his silent nephew began their preparations for lunch.
A very large loaf, goats' cheese, olives and dark red wine
were produced from a cupboard and Niko had started to
cut great slices of bread before we left the jetty. I think we
all rather envied them that simple meal, knowing that
Tracy had something of an obsession concerning lobsters.

It was nearly 3 p.m. when we began to follow blindly in
her footsteps, trudging from one small hotel to another,
realising it was getting late for lunch of any kind. At the
fourth hotel we did not bother to follow her inside but
humbly waited in a queue on the sand track as the quest
for *langouste* began yet again.

Mrs Prothero was the first to voice a complaint. "Who's
over-fond of the sound of her own voice? It's too bad. I'm
hungry."

From the hotel I heard Tracy using the phrase which
seems to occur in so many French conversations: *"Pas
très cher?"*

Jane nudged me and whispered, "Things went from bad
to worse." She giggled. "It's absurd. Us all standing around
like this. Like, what's that Laurel and Hardy word, like
chumps."

Tracy appeared smiling and waving her hands above her head like a victorious boxer. "I've had to give up on the old lobster. Seems to be a shortage. He says he has some very fresh fish. Caught half-an-hour ago. Big fish. They'll have to be cooked so it means a wait, okay? A nice clean kitchen. . . ."

A taller than average Greek in a dazzling white suit appeared by her side, smiling and welcoming us. We all pushed quickly along the path leading round the hotel to a terrace where tables were positioned to look out over the sea. Two boys emerged to lay the tables with snowy white cloths and then brought baskets of bread, plates of black olives and bottles of white wine. We all began a biblical snack with wine. Chatter and laughter broke out. Bottles were quickly emptied and replaced. The wine was delicious : dry, with a distinctive nutty flavour, something like a Sancerre, arriving at the table in greenish-yellow bottles misted from a sojourn in ice. We were seated under a vine arbour that protected us from the glaring sun. One other customer, a stout bald gourmet, was taking his time over a flaky pastry concoction.

After a few glasses of wine I looked at the motley crew of the yacht *Freedom*, experiencing a rather pleasant feeling of togetherness. It was a predictable symptom, as Dorothy would say, to be followed by a surge of amorousness; to which I would have had to plead guilty, knowing myself just as well as Dorothy did; my defence was that too much drink did not make me aggressive or rude or sick —just friendly and amorous.

I stood up, brandishing an empty bottle, saying, "And he called for stronger wine." Jane threw a crust of bread which just missed me and when I sat down she tapped the back of my left hand with a fork. "Now behave."

"Just enjoying myself," I said, and thought I detected the very faintest slurring.

"I know. It's super here. But those boys may think you're being funny at their expense. I'm sure they don't speak a word of English. And what service! Imagine arriving at a comparable place in England at 3.15 for lunch and getting a welcome like this. Fabulous!"

Another bottle appeared before us and we toasted each other, Mrs Merchant at the next table who produced a delightful smile, and the old bald gent who responded by raising his coffee cup.

Amongst a good deal of laughter and happy chatter there seemed to be only one dissident voice. Tracy appeared to be on edge about the time being taken to cook the fish, or perhaps she was alarmed at the great quantities of wine being consumed. Mrs Merchant said, "I'm sure they're trying," and Tracy replied, "Trying—yes, like trying to commit suicide with Junior aspirin."

Jane turned in her chair to talk to Hildegarde, rested her right hand lightly on my left arm and left it there, an understated intimacy that seemed to have some significance. Once again I was aware of her fresh, unspecific scent. Her sun-glasses had been replaced by half glasses on a steel frame but I was not sure whether they were to be used to study the non-existent menu or just to beguile me. When she turned again I looked into her brown eyes and felt that the moment had arrived for some fairly honest talking. I told her about my wife who liked living in the country, being awakened by the dawn chorus, wild flowers, long walks, gardening and vegetarian meals. I told her I was a much less satisfactory character, desperately short of inner resources, easily bored, with idiosyncratic tastes. I probably told her a good deal more of which I was not aware. Who knows how much we tell by gestures, sighs, fleeting expressions?

Jane said, "Your wife sounds very nice and sensible. Why isn't she here?" I told her that Dorothy did not like sun-and-sea holidays, and was on a walking tour in Iceland. At that moment we both smelt fried fish and saw a large dish being placed in front of Mrs Merchant and Mrs Prothero.

Jane sniffed. "Boy, that smells good. You wait, any

moment now someone's going to say 'This is the life'." She took another drink, looked at me reflectively as if coming to some decision, and told me that her family lived in Yorkshire, that she had two brothers who were farmers, that she had spent "five hateful years at a boarding school", that she now lived in London and was in between jobs, hoping for one in the BBC. I told her that I lived mainly in my flat above my small bookshop. I told her that there was no instrument in the world sufficiently sensitive to measure the importance of my bookselling activities.

Jane laughed and said, "I live near a Duke Street too. But not your S.W.1 one. Spanish Place. Do you know it?"

"Yes, side of the Wallace Collection."

The fish intended for us arrived. It was indeed large, fried crisp on the outside and smelling of fennel. There was a salad of tomatoes, cucumber, artichokes and lettuce. Also a dish of sliced boiled potatoes, brushed with oil and speckled with herbs. As Jane helped herself I overheard a brief exchange of words between Hildegarde Wegel and Dave Haswell, puzzling in its simplicity, as if it must have some coded significance.

Jane took a mouthful of salad, wrinkled her nose and said "This is the life", grinning in a fetching way. Intimacy still seemed to be growing between us in swift, imperceptible stages. At the same time I was aware how foolish I was to embark on another lop-sided friendship which could only end in sadness. The ego eagerly brings bad news to which the id does not wish to listen. As Jane talked about eating out in London I was covertly studying her. Her very white teeth, a tiny scar on her cheek that looked as if it might have been made by a fish-hook, her clear mid-brown eyes, her way of looking round at everything with pleasure. She possessed an elemental sense of freshness and surprise that I had long ago lost.

I had drunk much too much wine. There was no doubt about that. I had thought the food might have a sobering effect but I was feeling steadily more vague and had to concentrate hard, like Mrs Findlay-Duncan, to make sense of what Jane said about eating sesame seed and buckwheat at some place called the Nuthouse in Kingly Street.

When the fish was finished we both decided against any of the flaky pastries which were being offered as sweets. I saw Tracy get up and go into the restaurant. After a few moments I followed her, entering a small washroom to splash my face with cold water. When I came out, still rather fuddled, Tracy was talking to the proprietor, querying some entry on a long bill. I handed her a bundle of drachmas, telling her I was paying for two lunches.

It was a stifling, oppressive afternoon and from the back door of the hotel I could see hot air looking like a trembling curtain. It was pleasant to enter the shade of the arbour again, but I was not happy to see that Jane had moved down the table in my absence to sit with the young trio. I watched them enviously, thinking that they were all on the same wave-length while my receiver was usually tuned in to old stations. They wouldn't remember Radio Luxembourg and AFN.

Yes, I'm old, I thought. Older than Donald Duck. Possibly older even than Mickey Mouse. I stumped off down the sandy path on what seemed to be wooden legs. I was equipped for a swim, wearing swimming-trunks beneath my shorts, and I thought I had better have one. I could remember when a quick-dip had done wonders in sobering me up during a wine-tasting trip in Yugoslavia.

"Harry! Wait a moment." I turned to see Andrew Foster following me. Swinging his binocular and camera cases, he looked rather like a stage drunk in a Somerset Maugham play about Malaya, wearing slightly over-long tennis shorts. He said confidentially, "Do you feel perhaps something's going on here—something you and I don't know about?" Squinting slightly in the glaring sunlight gave him an odd look of cunning.

"What do you mean?"

"Can't put my finger on it. But something . . . 'Bout that bunch back there. Int'resting . . . Something."

Two chumps, I thought, standing in the blazing sun, talking fuddled nonsense.

"No, sorry, I don't know what you mean. Just going along the cliff to find somewhere to swim. Coming?"

"Later, old man, later. Must take some snaps of this place first. Weren't we lucky? Delicious meal I thought. If only old Evstratios could cook like the chef here!"

"Yes. But then we'd be paying twice the money at Theo's. Well, I'll see you. Tracy said we have one hour 'free time' before sailing back. Okay?"

After Foster had retreated, fiddling with his camera case, I felt momentarily depressed and lacked the will to move. Dorothy is right, I thought, I am a failure. Here I am at forty-six and no idea what I shall do when I grow up. These trips I make are just futile attempts to escape from myself. I remembered something damning that Jane had said about Tracy: "She lives in a world of make-believe. Very impermanent."

Laughter and happy young voices coming from the arbour drove me further along the cliff path. I brooded for a minute on what Foster had said, remembering the curious, laconic exchange between Haswell and Hildegarde, then gave up trying to make sense of his suspicions. It was too hot and I was too drunk for mental investigations.

After a few minutes I reached a good spot for diving. It was quite high but the water was clear and deep. There were some steep sandstone ledges which I could use to haul myself out and scramble back up the cliff.

My dive was not at all fancy as I was anxious to hit the area which I could see was free from rocks. Swooping down, I mentally framed the epitaph "Drunk 'n' Diving". The anticipated rush and roar of entry into the sea was strangely muted, like a dream dive. I went down a long way, still as if diving in a dream, till I reached an icy vein of water and then had to consciously struggle up to reach the surface. In the shadow of the cliffs the sound of the sea and the seabreezes changed into runes charged with malevolent magic. Swimming seemed a great labour. I said "Stupid idiot" to myself and swallowed some water. But it was still like a dream, as if someone else was swimming badly and mistiming his breathing. My voice had sounded strange and quite alien.

Close to the stone ledges I saw they started slightly higher than I had thought when looking down. When I reached up my fingers were several inches short of the first ridge which would enable me to pull myself out. I slipped back into the sea, shooting a look upwards to see if there was anyone about to see my ludicrous performance. The cliff-top was empty. Death of an insignificant person, I thought. Or, death of the man from the doll's house shop—another headline for Mrs Prothero to remember.

I swam out a few yards and then back again, throwing myself up on the slippery stone with so much force that it knocked the breath out of me. This time the tips of my fingers were just an inch short of getting a grip. I remembered a satirical warning notice that had been posted up in mined areas in Korea : WITH CARE YOUR BODY SHOULD LAST YOU A LIFE TIME.

Treading water for a while, I surveyed the cliffs to see if there was another spot where I might clamber out but could not spot one more likely than the place I had already tried. It looked as if I was going to have a longish swim back to the beach where we had landed. I thought of Dolek's favourite saying, *"Nissayon Elohim"*, "God is testing me".

As I started rather wearily to swim out towards the headland and the next bay I heard some noise on the cliffs and looked up to see that most of the crew of *Freedom* were there, calling out and waving. I trod water and waved back, wishing that Jane was not going to witness my ignominious retreat. As I did so Dave Haswell took off his shirt and dived in with the minimum amount of splash. His crawl was very efficient and economical too. In a few moments he was within yards of me.

Momentarily his sea-green eyes looked monstrously enlarged as he raised his head. He gestured towards the ledges and said, "I thought those rocks looked like bad news." This immediate summing-up of the situation impressed me. "Bet you a grand it'll take a double act to get out of here. You swim up and I'll give you a shove."

When I attempted my third leap out of the sea Haswell caught my soles and pushed. My hands caught the ledge and I dragged myself out. Then I turned to give him a hand. There was some laughter and ironic applause from the cliff-top crowd. As we slowly clambered up the cliff I thought that the incident was hardly likely to commend me to Haswell as a member of his treasure-hunting team.

THE JOURNEY BACK from Sidari was swifter and
more dramatic than the trip in the morning. We travelled
non-stop to Nissaki under an evening sky which seemed to
change colour continuously as a strong wind sprang up.
There was an extraordinary incandescent sunset and then
bat's wing darkness through which we sped with a full set
of straining sails and hissing petrol lamps.

When Niko and his nephew had been thanked and
tipped we all hurried up to our rooms to shower and
change. While I was sitting on my bed putting on my socks
I could hear the wind in the cypresses sounding like the
long drawn out howling of wolves. Theo's Taverna was
strangely silent—so silent I could hear the dutiful beating
of my heart.

When I was ready to go down to dinner a muffled
swear-word next door sent me sneaking over to the thin
partition. I took down some broken phrases:

"Different strokes for different blokes."

"Wipe his nose for him."

"What do you want—a medal?"

"Tomorrow?"

"We'll see."

"I like it, I like it."

"We'll see, we'll see."

Their door slammed with a dramatic loudness, like an
exit in an amateur play. After a few minutes I followed
the Cockney treasure-hunters downstairs but there was no
sign of them; only Mrs Merchant standing out in the moonlight watching the wind tussling with the cypresses. Her
thin face in profile, one-eyed, looked like the Jack of
Diamonds.

The bar was half in darkness, and though it was late the usually protracted preparations for dinner did not seem to be in progress. It was as if our being away for lunch had disorganised Theo's small establishment. From the restaurant I heard a voice tinny with anger. I spied a man in the bar mirror looking wary and evasive, then I saw Mrs Findlay-Duncan struggling to open the glass door to the restaurant. She looked extremely tired if not ill, her dark eyes appeared cloudy and her hands trembled.

I opened the swing door and said good-evening to her. She stared at me as if I was unrecognisable and staggered past, muttering something to herself. Behind her I saw the General and Theo Mavromichalis. An unveiled look from the General's cold blue eyes made me feel I should be standing at attention or doing something more useful than opening doors. He nodded and hurried away without a sign of being crippled.

Theo came to my side still regarding the door through which the General had retreated. He said to me confidentially, "Evening Mr Gilm. The General, his lady. Today he take her all over island. . . ." He shook his head, making it sound a slightly disreputable episode.

Claude Montefiore was seated at an unlaid table, watching events above his newspaper, an habitual crafty look in his eyes.

Andrew Foster approached me, also looking at the still faintly swinging door. "Quite a chap, the General. You know—when father says turn we all turn. . . . Going to be quiet here tonight, old man. The youngsters are off to Ipsos to treat Tracy to a lobster dinner."

I absorbed this unwelcome news silently, nodding. Foster said, "I'll try to ginger things up a bit here—get them cracking. I think old Evstratios is one over the eight tonight."

As Foster walked over to the door leading to the kitchen I heard a commotion outside and walked back through the bar in case Mrs Findlay-Duncan had come to harm in her fuddled stupor.

Instead of the General's wife I found Dave Haswell brushing down his jeans with his hands and looking ruefully at a skinned elbow. "Those bleeding stone steps! It's true what they say—more haste less speed. Christ, I took a spill there mate! Night." He ran off waving.

A moment later I heard a burst of laughter, then Jane Mackmurdo calling out, "It's rich, isn't it?" followed by an exclamation in German. Then gleeful, shouting voices, hoots of derision, a car engine starting up, revving and rapidly accelerating to climb the hill. The moon had disappeared behind the massing clouds and I stared moodily at the limitless gloom. Ah, I thought bitterly, nice to be young and carefree and suddenly make up a late evening expedition to Ipsos, leaving all the old codgers behind.

The disorganisation of Theo's Taverna extended even to the absence of the usual canned *bouzouki* music. Instead there was the untuned blare of a radio station, then a breathy alto-sax rendering of "Stardust".

As I turned to go back to the restaurant there was a tiny chinking noise and I bent down to find that in his tumble down the steps Haswell must have lost a coin, a comb, and a piece of paper. Without hesitation I pocketed the scrap of paper and walked through the bar.

Seated at my table, I pretended to scrutinise the menu I knew by heart. It contained a short list of wines—Provata, Lavranos, Theotoki and Greek Domestica—which were usually available, and a longer selection of dishes which proved more elusive. I studied the selection of sweets with their added descriptions in English : "*Halva* (White flaky mixture made from sesame, honey and crushed almonds); *Yaourti* (Junket with cinnamon)", then took the slip of paper from my pocket and held it against the menu.

It was a letter-heading for a firm called "Phillips & Haswell, TV. HI-FI. ELECTRONICS" with an address in Praed Street. There were notes in two different hands.

Neatly written in a stylish script at the top was the name "Peter Lumke" and a phrase between quotation marks: ". . . as a cult will survive centuries after its myths have been exposed and its sources of faith tainted. . . ." Scribbled below this in pencil was a list of phrases: Rennes Pentagram Poussin painting The Circle The Eagle's Nest The Dead Man.

It was, as my mother would have described it, "a real conundrum". But I was unable to brood for long on this mysterious list as Andrew Foster came over to my table, obviously amused by something. "I was right," he said, nodding portentously. "Old Evstratios *is* out of action. Blotto. So Theo's cooking himself. An even simpler menu tonight! Choice of steak and chips—or, would you believe it, lobster!"

8

I TOOK THE measure of myself in Korea in 1951. At that time, Korea's rice-growing economy was built upon human excrement. Ox carts, piled high with small barrels, collected the sewage from every household. Eighty wen, roughly a penny ha'penny, was the going rate then for a barrel. So it was in what my friend Dusty Miller called "The glorious land of shit" that I learned some fundamental lessons about myself.

When we were training in England I had hated regimental soldiering while preserving the illusion that I should be better fitted once we went into action. But in action I learned the hard way that my greatest talent was for "keeping my head down". Strange that in all those months this never aroused any comment. In a hectic moment of hand-to-hand combat I knocked out a young Chinese soldier with my left hand, breaking his jaw, and this earned me the nick-name "Tarzan"; but there were no unfavourable words about my slowness at getting into action, my trick of hugging the ground, my deaf ear in at least one emergency.

Still in my dreams I march along the Main Supply Route north of Taegu, a terrible road with a litter of rust-red T34 tanks, smashed trucks, collapsed telegraph-poles and burnt-out shacks, an insane piling-up of destruction. Vivid still in my memory is the ironic notice warning of mines; a blood-red board with a skeleton in white and the words: YOU TOO CAN HAVE A BODY LIKE MINE.

The Chinese offensive over the Imjin River began in the evening of the 22nd April 1951. Very quickly the Belgians were attacked, by-passed and surrounded. The Chinese used their "sea-wave" tactics, the first indication of their attack being the blowing of whistles and horns. They chose the period of the full moon so that the outlines of peaks would guide their units roughly in the right direction, while other details of positions and movements could be given by signals on whistles and bugles. The Chinese advanced in massed waves, giving the daunting impression of unending reserves of troops.

As the battle went on and the Chinese pressure increased it was obvious that the enemy swing was towards the west and bearing hardest on us Gloucesters. During the night of the 23rd to the 24th April our battalion was shifted to the top of an L-shaped hill some two thousand yards south-west of our previous position. There we dug in and stayed for thirty hours.

When we were without food and very short of water and ammunition, a force of Filipino tanks and infantry, with some Eighth Hussar tanks, moved up to relieve us but were ambushed and forced to retreat.

At dawn on the 25th our position was desperate. There were about a hundred stretcher cases on the steep hill and helicopters could not land there. When the Chinese bugles and whistles signalled a fresh assault, Lieutenant-Colonel Carne ordered the drum-major to blow the "long reveille". Soon afterwards we were given permission to retreat but the Colonel and the Sergeant-Major stayed behind with the wounded.

I have two legacies from my stint in Korea. One is the memory of the Korean wind—that eerie, chill wind with its emanation of death—a dreadful shape that slowly materialises and then dwindles slowly into the distance. The other, more important, legacy is doubt about myself. In an emergency, faced with a life or death situation, could I act decisively—act with courage? No answer came the stern reply.

9

THEO'S TAVERNA, Nissaki, Corfu.
22nd September 1976.

I slept fitfully, waking to the sounds of creaking springs, muffled voices, and once to a burst of insane laughter, quickly stifled. Then a short, strange dream in which I was trying to buy the Jewish religious paraphernalia that Dolek Menkes had hoarded for so many years. The Seder plate, the Sabbath Menovah, the Nannukah lamp, the phylacteries and prayershawls in their embroidered velvet bags, the ethrog box and the gold Kidduch goblet—all the things which had ended up being pitched into a box at the Pimlico auction sale—in my dream they seemed infinitely desirable.

Dolek was obviously very ill and anxious not to part with life or his cherished belongings. There was no sympathy in me and I thought how strange it was that he should want to cling to life, even beyond hope. Nor would I take no for an answer about the bits and pieces, deviously trying to confuse the issue and keep him vague about exactly what I was buying.

I say a strange dream because while the dream-maker had got the cluttered details of Dolek's room just as it had been during his last weeks at home, and the airless sick-room atmosphere, and the smell of the medicine he took for the cough he was never going to cure, I wanted to protest at the new character assigned to me. At the same time I felt moved by some obscure grievance against Dolek and as if I were suffering from an indefinable malaise.

The old man shut his eyes wearily and his dry lips moved silently. I stared up at a long crack that meandered across the dusty ceiling, indifferent to his plight, full of professional cunning and cajolery. Dolek gave a weary groan and his face was suddenly covered with black webs of shadow. I moved to the window, a close-up of biscuit-coloured bricks blackened with grime and the oblique view down into Old Pye Street. My face reflected in the window was set in a judicial grimace.

I woke from the bad dream with a jerking movement of my head, determined to escape from its sinister hold. I glanced at my watch to see that it was 7 a.m., the hour that army service had forever ordained as marking the limit of my sleeping time. Something about the atmosphere of Theo's Taverna made me feel that my watch was wrong and that it must be much earlier. I experienced a quickening of the senses together with a strange feeling of inertia. I lay like an invalid trying to divine what was going on that was different. Smells and noises, I thought. Usually at seven I could smell coffee being brewed and bread baking, something at which old Evstratios excelled. This morning there were no such smells. Noises too were different. Usually, first thing in the morning, I could hear a quiet conversation between the amiable, small, plump maid called Asimeni and a nameless girl who sometimes worked in the kitchen with Evstratios. This morning it sounded more like a Greek opera. Two bass voices shouting, two or three exuberant sopranos jabbering. Even the periods of silence had a dramatic quality, as one felt they presaged another burst of excited shouting. The first scream got me out of bed and I walked out on to the communal balcony indifferent to any intrusion on Hildegarde Wegel's privacy.

Immediately below I saw Theo and Evstratios apparently having an argument with a great deal of gesticulation. Evstratios turned away after making a movement illustrating frustration and anger, and his dark face looked like a Byzantine ikon. Theo started to walk away and then broke into a run. Some more screaming, and I decided to dress without shaving and see what was going on.

People who usually rose later than myself had been wakened by the screams too, and I saw Mr and Mrs Merchant in pyjamas and nightdress walking along the passage. Mrs Merchant said, "Oh, so you're going down, Harry" in a tone that implied relief that I was there to deal with whatever was happening.

"Yes I am. Right away."

"Good. I think it's that sweet little girl, I think it's Asimeni who was screaming."

Hildegarde Wegel, in a wet bikini, her eyes wet with tears and her face contorted, ran up the stairs as I walked down them, brushing off a tentative hand with which I tried to restrain her.

When I got outside the taverna I could see Asimeni standing alone on the jetty looking out to sea. There was a great deal of unseen activity going on behind the taverna, with raised voices, exclamations and a car's engine being revved.

Asimeni wore her usual black dress with old pink slippers. Her body was shaking with emotion and when I got up close I smelt the raw onion odour of rank perspiration. I nervously put my hand on her shoulder. When she turned her face was crumpled and she made a ghastly choking noise like a child who has sobbed to a point beyond exhaustion. She looked at me, nodding and shaking silently for a few moments, unable to speak. Then she pointed out to sea where a large motor-boat was slowly making its way in to the tiny harbour. "The young men. The brave young men. Dead. Both dead."

A nervous spasm in my empty stomach made me feel slightly sick. Automatically I asked, "Which men?" but I had an unpleasant presentiment about her answer.

"The young men—they always sailing. See—their little boat."

Looking again at the motor-boat, I could see that a caique without a mast was being towed along behind it. A fisherman was standing in the launch, waving very slowly towards someone behind me. I turned and saw that it was Theo, holding his head with both hands. Mr Merchant, in a dressing-gown, came along the jetty and said, "My God, this is a terrible, terrible business, Harry! Evstratios tells me those fine young boys have been drowned. Just awful."

Asimeni turned and ran back along the jetty towards the taverna. A small crowd had accumulated there but they stood in silence. As the motor-boat came closer I could see there were indeed two bodies lying behind a coil of rope, one on a canvas tarpaulin and the other on a piece of old black mackintosh. Theo and Evstratios walked slowly towards the steps with morose, brooding expressions to give the fishermen a hand in lifting the bodies. Reluctantly I went forward too.

Dave Haswell was cradled comfortably in the tarpaulin and at first glance might have been asleep, but Ken Reardon lay awkwardly on the unyielding mackintosh and a movement made his arm fall limply down. His hair was plastered across his face, and his mouth was half open. Salt glittered on his cheeks which were a dough-grey colour. There was a vivid bruise on Haswell's neck; his large green eyes were open and staring unfocused like a blind man's. When we had got the bodies to the top of the steps we all paused, as if seeking guidance as to what to do next. At that moment Asimeni came running up with two towels which she laid over the faces of the drowned men, then with simple dignity she made the sign of the cross above them.

10

A DAY OF VENETIAN blue and gold. The sky a flat blue wash; the sun a white gold blaze upon half-closed eyelids. After a long swim Jane and I lay prone with faces down, on towels very close to the sea's edge. All the temporary residents of Theo's Taverna had been instructed by Tracy to remain within call as the police were expected to question us about what we knew of the movements of the drowned men on their last day. I had not seen Haswell and Reardon after lunch on the day they went off so my contribution was unlikely to be helpful, but I felt guilty about my secret knowledge of their treasure-hunting activities, and the possession of Haswell's notes, ominously ending in "The Dead Man", which now were hidden in my paperback copy of *Middlemarch*.

The swim, the extreme heat, and a general mood of depression in Nissaki all had an enervating effect. Jane and I talked on trivial topics. She seemed as anxious as I was to avoid the subject of the tragedy. She told me that her favourite book was *The Wind in the Willows* and her favourite character was Ratty. I chose Toad. "You would," she said provocatively, "I can just hear you saying Poop-poop!" It was an amiable insult, particularly as it was accompanied by a smile.

Jane's light brown hair, which had clung to her head like a dark brown cap when we emerged from the sea, was now becoming its natural colour and springing into delightful little curls. It would have been easy to stare at them like a love-sick youth or to reach out and touch them, but I restrained myself. She told me that if she got a job in the BBC it would be as a secretary, but that she hoped to get into production one day. "Documentaries—facts are more interesting than fiction. Nearly anything factual can be presented in an interesting way." Then she asked me who ran the bookshop in Mason's Yard while I was away and I told her I had a spinster assistant called Mary Carpenter, and that the shop's turnover usually went up in my absence. I told her that I had a cat living on the premises too.

Jane raised her head at that, frowning. "Don't know that I approve of cats living in London flats. Litter boxes and so on. Poor thing—like being in prison."

"Not at all. Magoo is never confined. He goes out over the roofs. For all I know he spends his nights in St James's Palace."

"You take a chance in letting him out."

"He takes his chances. We all take our chances. Do you know that saying 'To touch the knee of the wife of your best friend is dangerous but to love at all is dangerous and what is dangerous is exciting'?"

"That's not a saying! You've just made that up! Haven't you? Admit it."

"I may have done. Every four or five years I do make up something like that."

She looked at me closely, her gaze travelling from my face to my hands which were practically in the sea. She said, "They're strong hands, but not particularly capable looking. . . ."

"That's the story of my life."

Jane lifted herself up slightly to lazily fling a stone into the waves. There was the merest fuzz in her armpit. The stretching movement of arm, breast and throat seemed to have something of beauty in it. It was easy to joke about touching knees but I realised she might not want any physical approaches from a middle-aged man, and I wanted to keep our friendship even if it was always to be on a platonic level. I removed myself from temptation by standing up and looking along the beach.

Near the stone wall of the jetty Andrew Foster was

talking animatedly with one of the Corcyra Holiday Tours'
top brass, a heavily built man with a Nero haircut. I saw
Foster outlining a map or diagram in the air while Nero
haircut nodded sagaciously.

Jane had not moved from her towel. She said im-
periously, "Whatever you're doing, stop it! Come back
here. I haven't finished with you yet. You've got nice feet
but otherwise there's room for improvement."

I lay down again promptly. Doing what you're told is
not so bad when a beautiful girl is giving the orders. Jane
grimaced and said, apropos of nothing, "So many marriages
do seem to fritter themselves away."

I thought, touché pussy-cat, but kept silent. I closed my
eyes. After two bad nights it would have been very easy to
nod off there, lulled by the unending sound of the sea and
gentle sea-breezes. Instead I made an effort to keep awake
by telling Jane about my daughter Judith, how she had
shown, quite early on, a freakish scientific ability, about her
successful career as a research chemist and of her present
job with a great chemical organisation in Hamburg. I
rattled on a bit but I could tell from Jane's responses that
she was not bored.

Then an unwelcome intrusive noise on the beach. Our
small private world at the sea's edge was being invaded.
I looked round to see that Andrew Foster and Nero haircut
were approaching in a purposeful way, Foster diplomatically
trudging noisily.

Nero haircut said, " 'Morning, Miss Mackmurdo...
Mr Gilmour... Short conference... In the bar... Few
minutes' time... No need to dress... Quite informal."

The staccato phrases went with an odd, impersonal
delivery, as if he was hardly involved with what was going
on. "My name's Woollard—Peter... Hugh Morley, Corcyra's General Manager... Flown over too... In there
now... Talking to the police."

We got up and ambled towards the taverna. Jane touched

the strap of her dark brown bikini and asked, "You're sure this is all right? I could change in five minutes."

"Really no need . . . Others won't . . . Very sad affair . . . But *you* are on holiday . . . Hugh's put that point quite forcibly . . . The police see that."

We all nodded. Woollard said, half to himself, "Yes, tragic . . . And timing most unfortunate." We all shot a look at him, but he had only put into words a thought that must have lurked in other minds as it had in mine. It was the 24th September. Our package tour holiday was planned to end with a charter flight back to Heathrow the following afternoon. We must all have wondered if we should now be on this flight or whether the police would insist on us staying while they conducted their investigation into the tragic accident. Another group of Corcyra Holiday Tours customers, destined to stay at Theo's Taverna, would be arriving on the plane scheduled to take us back. If we had to remain on Corfu, then there was the dismal possibility of our being put into strange lodgings in the town. Such trivial, selfish thinking was behind my reluctance to mention what I had overheard to the police.

Andrew Foster opened his mouth to say something but then thought better of it. After a few moments he said banally, "I see they're all there."

We filed slowly into the bar where the others were waiting silently. Tracy, Theo, Evstratios, Asimeni and the nameless maid stood in a separate group. I had found Greek names difficult to disentangle because of their habit of using *paratsouklia*, or nicknames. A wireless somewhere was chattering away in Greek while another quieter Greek conversation was taking place in the restaurant. The incomprehensible Greek language made me brood again anxiously on the possibility of an enforced prolonged stay. Cocooned by Corcyra Holiday Tours, spoonfed by Tracy, staying in Theo's Taverna where the staff had a working knowledge of English, one had the best of both worlds : all the pleasures of the Ionian Sea without having to battle with Greek lexicons. Immured in some small hotel in Corfu town, waiting for the arrival of the C.I.D. from the mainland, would be a very different matter.

I looked round at my fellow guests, wondering how they felt about such a prospect. Mrs Prothero, clad in a shimmering silk garment, was seated, closely studying a document. Tracy and Hildegarde both looked pale and as if they had been crying recently. Hildegarde wore a white towelling gown and her hair was dragged back unflatteringly in two clumps. Tracy wore a sun-dress instead of her usual T-shirt and jeans; her makeup was much more restrained than usual, with a beneficial effect. Mr and Mrs Merchant were whispering together in a concerned way, but I imagined that might well be to do with the possibility of alterations to complicated connecting flight plans. Claude Montefiore was playing an endless game with a Gauloise packet. Theo was sweating visibly; he wore a white shirt, a narrow black tie and a navy suit jacket with slightly-over-long black trousers; he had the hopeful, unwanted air of an undertaker. Evstratios was in his white chef's garb, looking ill-at-ease; his dark eyes moved round ceaselessly, waiting for reactions, as if searching for a clue as to how to behave.

A tall, energetic-looking man emerged from the restaurant. He appeared like someone who might be an executive for a more high-powered organisation than Corcyra Holiday Tours. He said, with an expression finely judged to mix welcome with sadness, " 'Morning everybody! I'm Hugh Morley. Sorry that we should meet in such sad circumstances. And indeed that your holiday should end like this. First of all I'm sure you will want to know that we are doing everything in our power for the families of the young men concerned. Naturally we have offered to fly them out here—and so on."

Morley paused, unrolling a map, and two uniformed policemen emerged from the restaurant. They both had watchful eyes. One stood with his arms akimbo; the other

59

clutched a manilla folder and an unruly sheaf of onionskin paper. Morley looked round at the policemen and introduced them—"Lieutenant Troupakis, Sergeant Venizelos". They nodded and smiled gravely.

Morley shot Troupakis a questioning look, then proceeded slowly. "This was a very great misfortune, but as far as we can see no one really was to blame. Just a stroke of terribly bad luck. As I understand it, the young men were last seen going off in their caique about 5.30 p.m. I believe you saw them then, Mr Merchant?"

"I did, sir. In fact I had a few words with them—but nothing of importance. . . ."

"Well, if you can remember, I think. . . ."

"Just, oh just. . . ." Mr Merchant looked round at me, slightly embarrassed. "Well, as I recall we had a little joke. About Mr Gilmour here getting rather merry at Sidari the other day, jumping in the sea there and then having difficulty getting out again. You see, Dave Haswell dived in to help him."

"I see. So, as they went off at five-thirty everything was quite normal?"

"Oh yes."

Morley held up a large-scale map of Corfu. I had studied the one I had borrowed again from Andrew Foster till I felt that I knew every inch of it. In outline it resembled a leg; Nissaki was in the thigh area and the town of Corfu near to the back of the knee. Morley said, "You all know that the bodies were found by a fisherman setting out from Kouloura. The accident must have taken place off Karagol Point." He hesitated, pursing his lips. "Of course, with hind-sight one has 20–20 vision." He flicked a glance in Tracy's direction. "Possibly they might have been warned that some places in Kalami Bay are tricky for underwater swimming, but they were apparently very strong swimmers and experienced at scuba diving. Exactly why they should have been diving off Karagol Point is something we shall probably never know."

Henry Merchant made a diffident contribution, "As I recall, they weren't wearing their wetsuits."

"That's right. Their wetsuits were in their room. No doubt, however, that they were diving. They were found tangled up in a rope ladder, and both of them were wearing scuba equipment. What happened? I can only offer an informed guess that possibly one of them got trapped under water and the other became exhausted getting him free. . . ." Morley looked round the room, "We can take it then that no one here saw them after Mr Merchant?" There was a chorus of muttered "Nos". Hildegarde Wegel did not reply or shake her head, but stared fixedly at Morley with a look that used to be classified in the Army as "dumb insolence". The policemen talked quietly in Greek. Morley seemed to be pleased by the direction of their remarks and unwilling to say anything which might change it.

I was wondering again whether to say anything about the result of my eavesdropping. It could not possibly help the drowned men or their families; that was certain. Keeping quiet would compound a sense of guilt but I hated the idea of being singled out by Troupakis and Venizelos as a vital witness for the inquest, the one person who could give a reason for the mysterious diving off Karagol Point.

Mrs Merchant whispered to me, "The coach has certainly turned back into a pumpkin." I nodded. I had the strange feeling that I was the cynosure of more than one pair of eyes, in fact that I was under close observation. When Merchant had recalled the ludicrous incident at Sidari, I had felt free of selfconsciousness, but now that the interview with the police seemed to be coming to an end was I being watched for my reactions?

Troupakis rattled off a longish comment to Venizelos, so quickly that it sounded like a burst of light machine-gun fire. Venizelos shrugged and put his onionskin papers into the file. Troupakis made a salute-like gesture to us and the two policemen went back into the restaurant and seated themselves at a table covered with other papers.

Morley looked after them and let out a long breath. He was obviously relieved. The truth was probably that most of us were relieved. The sad affair was going to be dealt with efficiently and we were not going to be involved. We exchanged sheepish looks. Only Hildegarde Wegel wore a grimace that seemed to express a cosmic melancholy.

11

Lᴵᴸᴸᴵᴾᵁᵀ Hᴏᵁˢᴱ Mason's Yard, S.W.1.

27th September 1976.

My alarm clock has become dissolute and eccentric in middle-age, like its owner. Its call is feeble and erratic. What it really likes to do is to fall over. At 6.45 a.m. it began to dance about on the polished top of my bedside table, banging into the paperback *Middlemarch*, but as soon as I reached out it fell over into silence.

I got out of bed with a renewed enthusiasm for my routine, the predictable result of a trip abroad. Within fifteen minutes I had showered, shaved and dressed. I grated a Bramley cooking-apple and made some *muesli* with the apple, porridge oats, sultanas and cream. While the coffee was brewing I went into my tiny office-cum-study to look at the letters and papers which Mary Carpenter had set out neatly on the desk. Seeing that I had only been away for two weeks, there had been quite a satisfactory haul of cheques and orders. Mary had dealt with most of the orders, making a careful note on each one.

Thumbnail portrait of Mary C. Energetic, sensible, enthusiastic. Aged 51. Height 5 ft. 7 in. Slim build. Excellent teeth, nicely shaped mouth, attractive greying dark hair, yet somehow lacking in feminine allure. Eminently equipped to make a good career in a more important business, she fortunately has a strong interest in books. Fortunately too she has a small income that allows her to live reasonably despite the poor wage she gets from me. She is much better at dealing with customers than I am, she has a more genuine interest in their "wants"; and, a great prize, she understands financial matters and can make sense of a balance-sheet, something that I've never mastered.

Most of my Sunday had been spent in a long Thames-side walk from Woolwich to the Dartford tunnel, during which I'd decided that there was nothing I could do about the tragedy in Nissaki except return the piece of paper belonging to Dave Haswell. It could be done at once, anonymously, by post. I had been through all my letters immediately I returned from Corfu on the Saturday evening, but two items were worthy of a second reading: a coloured postcard from Iceland showing "The Gryta geyser" and, overleaf, some lines in a familiar hand:

Dear H. Back to the old routine eh! I am on the south coast. Delightfully cool weather after England's strange tropic summer. Scaled Hekla, more of a volcanic ridge than a true mountain with alpine ice-fields on its northern slopes. Then a tricky bit along the glacier river Markarfljot. Shall stay with Judith from 25th Sept. for a week/ten days. Dare I then visit dreaded London for a day or two on way back? Sure you're bronzed. Hope you're fit & happy. Food here grim. Love D.

I took another postcard to study again as I had my breakfast. It showed a view of the foyer of Sigmund Freud's house in Vienna, a very light room with white paint and walls that appeared to be panelled in yellow linen. Two hats and an overcoat belonging to the great man still hung on pegs along with a white-handled walking-stick. Two battered trunks and a travelling-bag stood in the hall; there was a wall-map of Vienna and an umbrella stand. The writing on the card resembled my own but was smaller and more legible:

Dearest Daddy,
Lightning hol. here before Mummy comes to stay in H. Why don't you come too? You are Jung enough to turn over a new leaf you know. (Jung) "... he anticipated the existentialists in insisting the search for mean-

ing in life is of central significance in human striving."
You would like Vienna. Why have you never been?
Strange chap my dad! Nevertheless, and perhaps
because, lots and lots of love from Judith.

The impulse to pack a bag and fly to Hamburg was
strong for a few minutes. I could afford to do it. My business, small and humble though it was, was doing well
enough under Mary's pertinacious attention. I missed talking to Judith, though undoubtedly we should get on each
other's nerves after a short stay; too much alike to live in
proximity. Could I discuss the matter of the Nissaki tragedy
with her, would she be appalled by all my eavesdropping?

The double rat-tat of the postman brought my brooding to an end. The reduced weekend activity of the Post
Office inevitably means that the Monday post is the smallest
of the week, usually only second-class matter that was not
delivered on the Saturday. Still, I hurried down to see
what had fallen into the net. There is a strange vein of
optimism in my pessimistic nature which shows itself particularly in relation to the post. Daily I have expectations
which are dashed.

The yield on the mat was about average for a Monday:
four auction catalogues, three booksellers' lists, two bills, a
circular in Japanese which would hit the waste-paper basket
promptly, and one letter which I saw had been posted in
London on Saturday evening. The pale blue envelope was
addressed in violet ink in a feminine, scrawling hand.
Optimistically I imagined it might be a billet-doux from
an actress I had met at a party six months previously.

I tore up the circular from Tokyo and dropped everything else apart from the letter on to my desk. The azure-
coloured envelope I took through to the kitchen, leaving it
unopened, savouring pleasurable anticipation as I poured
a second cup of coffee. It was made of unusually thick
hand-made paper and smelt as if it had been kept in a
drawer with face-powder.

65

When I opened the envelope two small printed slips fell out and fluttered to the ground. There were only a few lines scrawled over one page but they held my attention:

The Nissaki Tragedy. If you would search for the Explanation then you must inquire about the demented friends of the late Mr Townshend. Only by finding them will you understand what happened. But beware of the friends of the late Mr Townshend!

I was puzzled and disturbed by this strange anonymous letter and it was a few moments before I picked up the two slips which had been enclosed with it. One was plainly a cutting from a newspaper obituary column: TOWNS-HEND.—On 28th June 1976, suddenly in Geneva, Victor Mons Ormond Townshend.

The other snippet I recognised as being cut from *Who's Who*:

TOWNSHEND, Victor Mons Ormond, b. 7 September 1914; son of late Colonel Jervis Archibald Ormond Townshend D.S.O., and Ismay, 2nd d. of Sir W. Coupar. Address: Old Court, Toller Parva, Dorchester, Dorset.

From time to time I consult my battered, out-of-date copy of *Who's Who*, so I knew that this was an unusually modest entry. Most people tend to spread themselves about their education, publications, recreations and clubs, sometimes occupying a whole column or more.

I opened the office window wide and surveyed the familiar roof-top view where the odd washing-line and television aerial, anarchically askew, made the elegant turrets and casements of old town houses look like part of an Indian city. As I stared out my mind was struggling to make sense of the letter. Could it be possible that simply by finding the friends of the late Mr Townshend, who had keeled over in Geneva in June, I should understand how Haswell and Reardon had come to die off Karagol Point in September? It was quite as likely that the letter which accused Mr Townshend's friends of being demented came from someone who was herself unhinged. I examined the piece of blue paper again and wondered what a handwriting expert would make of that childish scrawl, the circular dots and the over-large exclamation mark. But writers of anonymous letters surely did not usually send material to give credence to their accusations; the obituary clipping must have been carefully preserved for three months.

My mind was going round and round the problem without making any headway, so I washed up, made my bed and did some general tidying. Putting some shirts into a bag to take to the laundry, the ghost of a smell of *ambre solaire* wafted me back to the beach at Nissaki. I should probably always associate its smell with that place and particularly the enjoyable hour I had spent there talking to Jane Mackmurdo.

"Hello! Harry?"

I walked downstairs to find Mary Carpenter reaching into our display window to rearrange a book. She was as enthusiastic as usual and normally I found her attitude stimulating, but my mind was still obsessed with the accusation against Mr Townshend's friends. Mary told me that my cat Magoo had not missed a single meal parade while I had been away, but probably missed me as he had made an unusual fuss of her. She also told me what had happened in the shop, and particularly of a nibble we had received from a Canadian librarian who had read of the Dolek Menkes Russian pamphlets. I nodded at regular intervals but I was thinking how to tackle a matter which I found much more absorbing. Suddenly it came to me that I should visit the electrical shop in Praed Street. In the circumstances it would be quite natural that I should go round there and tell Dave Haswell's partner how upset we had all been by the tragedy. Once I had thought of this idea my impulsive nature decreed that it should be done at once, and I felt impatient as Mary went on with her blow-by-blow account. Eventually I mentioned an auction sale that I had to view before lunchtime.

12

Getting off a bus near St Mary's Hospital in Praed Street I saw the Phillips & Haswell shop, next to two second-hand clothes shops standing side by side, their adjacent windows hung with dark jackets like funeral mutes shoulder to shoulder.

Mary Carpenter would have thought the TV window display hopelessly slack. The brown linoleum on which the sets stood was dusty, one price ticket had fallen over and another lay face down on the floor; a single strand of tinsel was looped along the top of the window, apparently left over from Christmas decorations. The interior was much the same, giving a daunting impression of a small stock, a couldn't care less attitude and approaching bankruptcy. No assistant appeared when the door-bell announced my entrance, and I stood by the counter for a few minutes before I heard someone moving slowly about behind a partition. Waiting there I felt awkward, like a man who has no natural manners and has to feel his way carefully. I was playing a part, feigning a deep sympathy I did not feel, not a very pleasant thing to do where death and mourning were involved.

I cleared my throat twice and then tapped on the counter before a door opened in the partition. A woman in her mid-fifties, wearing a flowered overall and head-scarf, smoking a cigarette, came out. Her manner combined reluctance and impatience. She said "Yes?" in a way that would not have encouraged me to buy anything.

"Mrs Haswell? My name's Harry Gilmour. I was on holiday with Dave. In Corfu. . . ."

"No. I'm Mrs Phillips." She broke into my explanation hurriedly as if she did not want to hear any more of it.

"You want my daughter, Barbara. She's—Dave's wife. Upstairs. In the flat. The next door, that way."

"Will it be all right? To call there?"

"Oh yes. Expect she'll be glad to see you. There's an entry-phone. Okay?"

A moment later I was introducing myself again on the entry-phone. A slightly husky female voice said simply: "Come on up. I'm opening the door."

Red carpeted white steps led up to a glossy red inner door decorated with a gilt anchor. It was ajar so I knocked and walked in. A thin girl with short blonde hair appeared at the end of the corridor, saying, "Hello. I'm Barbara, Dave's wife. Come on through."

It was a brightly decorated room with lots of white paint that had not succumbed to the Praed Street dust. Barbara Haswell stood with her hands on her hips giving me a close inspection. She wore a dark blue blouse with white trousers. Her eyes were exotically made up and that contributed to her rather hard look. I had heard some taped preparatory-to-takeoff music when I walked along the passage but she touched a switch and it went off with a click. There was a large couch covered in blue linen and three easy chairs. She slumped down on the couch as I entered the room. "My mum rang from downstairs so I knew you were coming. You're just back from Corfu?"

"Yes, I was on the same package holiday deal as Dave, at Theo's Taverna. I wanted to say how sorry we all were. . . ."

"That's nice. Thanks. Would you like a cigarette?" She lit one as she spoke.

"No, thanks. I don't smoke. Did the company offer to fly you out? The Corcyra Holiday people, I mean. They said they would."

"They did. But there didn't seem much point, not yet anyway. It's undecided what's going to happen. About . . . the funeral. . . ."

Her expression puzzled me, it seemed more to indicate

bottled-up annoyance than sadness. She had a small mouth set in lines of discontent. She paused, obviously weighing up something in her mind, then said, "Some other bloke phoned. He must have been at that place too, a Mr Foster. Said he would probably look in some time. I thought that was good of him."

"Yes, Andrew Foster, a nice chap. I noticed him talking to Dave two or three times, they seemed to get on well. . . ."

Barbara Haswell pulled a wry face. "Dave had the knack of making people like him. It's a gift. It was easy for him."

"I had a rather special reason for coming here. I dived into the sea at Sidari, at a rather tricky spot—when I'd had quite a lot to drink. I wasn't in danger really . . . But anyway Dave probably thought I was. So he dived in straight away."

Barbara nodded but said nothing. I found this rather disconcerting. Her responses and the atmosphere of our conversation were different from what they should have been.

"We were all puzzled. . . . It was a bit of a mystery why they were diving there—at Karagol Point."

"No mystery about that," Barbara said quickly. "The explanation's just over there. Do you want to see?"

She walked across the room and opened a door into a smaller one fitted out like an office with a desk and steel filing cabinets. The walls were covered with maps, charts and photographs, many of which had been cut from newspapers.

"You see! That's why. Treasure mad, Dave was. Always was, as long as I knew him. But it got worse all the time, like an illness really. You might not believe it now, but that shop downstairs—it was my dad's business before he died—it was a real money-spinner once. Dave was a first-rate electrician too, could have done very well, but oh no, he wouldn't settle for just a good living. He had to find a flaming fortune! I should have known—when I very first knew him he had one of those metal detectors, used to spend hours mooching along the Thames at low tide. Then he got friendly with Ken and they couldn't seem to think about anything else. Lake Toplits, Inverary, the Black Prince, Captain Drew, Oak Island—you name it, I've heard of it."

"So there may be treasure off Karagol Point? That's very odd because I talked about this with an old chap called Evstratios. He's the cook at Theo's Taverna, but he used to be a fisherman. I asked him if there might be a wreck or something like that near Kouloura. He said no very definitely, and he's lived there all his life."

"Well, Dave wouldn't have spent all that cash on going there without a good reason, that's for sure. Still . . . Lately . . . He was very cagey. Like that." She made a movement with her fingers to illustrate a closing trap. "Something strange has been going on. . . ." She paused, giving me another thoughtful look, then swung round to point at the steel cabinets. "Some of that stuff might have gone," she airily stated. "We had a break-in here a week ago. Peculiar that was. At first it looked as if they hadn't taken anything. My bag was on the dressing-table with fifteen pounds in it. Some odds and ends of jewellery, too. Premium bonds. None of them touched. Still, I knew someone had been in here—things had been moved about and one drawer had been forced open."

"What did the police do?"

"Nothing, because I didn't tell them. Didn't want a bunch of coppers in here, tramping round, doing damn-all. Anyway what kind of a break-in is it, when nothing's been taken? You can't claim on the insurance for some old papers. And for all I know Dave might not have wanted them here. . . . Well, really I didn't know what to do so I didn't do anything. Thought I'd wait till he got back. . . ."

There was a mirror on the back of the office door and she studied her reflection with a look of cold detachment. She gestured at the map-covered wall. "Would you like to have a look there? Does it interest you? I'll make a cup of coffee. There's something I want to ask you."

There was a mass of material to be scanned, from a nineteenth-century woodcut showing Blackbeard's head hanging from a bowsprit to a large photograph of the remains of the Spanish galleon *Capitana*, from a diagram of a pirate's treasure-chest illustrating the cut-out steel grille used to cover the lock mechanism to an odd cutting from a newspaper: "PIRATE'S GHOST TO LEAD TREASURE HUNTERS—Woman Medium Said to Be the Contact— Hidden £300,000,000 to Undo the Evil of His Life—a German Yachtsman, Hubert Mazenick, announced that he was starting for Cocos Island, taking with him Margo Schneider, a girl spiritualist . . .", but nothing that I could find related to Corfu in any way.

When I went back into the living-room I could smell scent as well as the instant coffee. A strong, cloying perfume, the kind that used to be known in my army days as "a real cock-raiser". Barbara had made up her mouth with a bright pink lipstick. The coffee was in two large yellow cups on a low table pulled close to the couch. She gave me a shrewd, appraising look as I sat down. I could see she was formulating something to say so I kept quiet. The silence between us lengthened, became oppressive. There were subjects I wanted to avoid and I was on the point of commenting on a red lacquer Chinese dragon when she suddenly got up from the couch, pushing the table back so that some coffee was spilled.

"Oh sorry, sorry!" She walked over to a cocktail cabinet. "I know I'm all nerves this morning. But after that last week—then this morning I had a surprise packet. Do you want to see what some rotten bastard sent me?" She took a large white envelope from the cabinet. "Go on, have a look. Now tell me—did you know that blonde tart?"

The envelope contained three photographs of Dave Haswell and Hildegarde Wegel making love, lying on a towel on a beach. In one they both wore bathing costumes and Haswell was kneeling by Hildegarde who was lying on her back. In another they were both nude, embracing lying together. The third showed them joined in the sexual act. As I looked at their photographs I remembered the two of them exchanging a few words at Sidari, something about "Do you think there will be a nice beach here?", "Yes, I should think there will be a nice beach"; phrases so banal they had puzzled me at the time. I said rather reluctantly, "Yes, I did see her at Nissaki."

Barbara gave me a cold, impassive look, then said bitterly, "With boobs that size you could hardly help bumping into her." Her amber-coloured eyes flashed. "Christ, what a mug I was! Left here with two kids while the glamour boy goes off pulling bits of spare. Well, I'm glad now I didn't fly out. . . ."

I turned the white envelope over as I replaced the photographs to see the address. It was not in the violet writing of my anonymous correspondent but impeccably typed, with the print-like effect of an electric machine. "A sick thing to do, sending you that." It was a situation where one was forced into inanity, for I wanted to keep my thoughts largely to myself and say little. While I sat there, shaking my head like a mechanical toy in a shop window, I was wondering if the package could possibly tie in with "the demented friends of the late Mr Townshend".

"Well, now you'll understand why I've got mixed feelings about what's happened. Christ, what a week I've had! And the business is very dicey at the moment too, so Mum and I have got all that to sort out now."

I got up saying, "I'm very sorry," leaving the envelope on the couch. "I'd like to help—if you can think of any way. . . ." I gave her one of my cards. "Give me a ring if you do. Knowing Nissaki and the Corcyra set up, I may be of some use."

"Okay, I might do that. Very kind of you to offer. We'll have to see." As she walked with me to the upstairs front door her mood seemed to have changed. She examined the card, saying "Yes, I might give you a ring. Don't want to be a nuisance, but. . . ." Her nervousness seemed to have been replaced by a bargaining manner. She held the card up elegantly between her thumb and index finger like a conjuror preparing to do a trick. Her nails seemed very long and meticulously kept for someone who had to look after two children and help in a shop. Now that she was calm I had the strong impression that she was clever and well able to look after herself.

At the bottom of the stairs I turned to wave goodbye. She waved back, calling out, "If you find the treasure you'll cut me in, won't you?" and disappeared behind the red door.

AFTER LEAVING PRAED Street I called in at Hodgson's book auction rooms in Chancery Lane. Afterwards I did some shopping on the walk from Fleet Street and when I returned to Mason's Yard I was carrying all I required for a simple lunch at home: a wholemeal loaf, tomatoes, Cox's Orange Pippins, Normandy butter and a Camembert from Paxton & Whitfield in Jermyn Street.

Turning in from Duke Street, I saw a man peering into my shop window. There was something familiar about his stocky build and slightly hunched shoulders. His rather apprehensive attitude was par for the course outside Lilliput House. Punters often made a tentative approach and a rapid retreat like fish easily frightened away from the bait. Looking in a window where there is only a bust of Shakespeare carved by William Perry from Herne's Oak, a poor but not particularly cheap copy of the 1678 *Pilgrim's Progress*, and a handful of Russian pamphlets tends to discourage all but confirmed bibliophiles.

As I got closer I saw who it was wearing the old-fashioned linen jacket and schoolboy grey worsted trousers.

"Hellow Andrew! Are you going to invest in some rare books?"

"Morning Harry. Don't like to waste your time, old man—if you're busy. Just wanted a chat."

"Entrey. The busy-ness is not terrific. At the moment all I'm going to do is to have a snack. Will you join me? Just bread and cheese but we could have some vino."

"Well, that's very kind."

Mary Carpenter came down from the office as we entered the shop and I introduced her to Foster and asked what she was doing about lunch. She said it was a yoghurt-

and-apple day and they had already been consumed. I left her chatting to Foster while I went down to the cellar where there were several hundred old books, wrapping paper, large balls of string and a few dozen bottles of wine. My hand generously hovered over one of three surviving bottles of Chambolle-Musigny, then commonsense prevailed and I picked up a Bulgarian Valtza Cabernet.

As we went up the stairs from the shop Andrew said, "Saw you had an old Bunyan edition in the window. Do you remember the names of his characters, 'Giant Despair' and 'Mr Steadfast'? I've always liked those names."

"Reminds me of you and that over-tall character in Nissaki."

Foster grinned at this slightly cheeky comment. As I laid the table in the kitchen my cat Magoo entered stealthily, saw I had a strange visitor and shot out again. We exchanged looks, mutely commenting on Magoo's wary behaviour, then Foster said, "My sister who lives in Islington met me at Heathrow and I'm staying with her for a few days. Funny thing, yesterday I was telling her about Corfu and suddenly I heard my voice like someone else's, droning and stumbling on, and I thought to myself, Christ, it's no wonder I couldn't get Harry interested. . . ."

"You mean when you spotted that 'giant' character?"

"Yes, and there was another occasion, old man. But I don't blame you." He looked round to make sure that the kitchen door was closed and went on in a slightly quieter voice : "It was my fault. My delivery's piss-poor. Yes, piss-poor. You know, I'd never heard that expression till we were in Nissaki but now it seems to be a very useful one. Anyway, I was lying on the beach one day and Haswell and Reardon walked past me, thinking I was asleep. I heard them say 'Do you think we'll make it?', 'I think our chances are piss-poor.' You must agree that was very odd seeing what happened, Harry."

I nodded as I eased the cork out of the bottle of Cabernet but said nothing. Years of running a one-man business had made me cagey and reluctant to take anyone into my confidence. Usually I preferred to tackle important matters alone, but I knew that the time had come to make a change. I could do with an ally in finding the treasure, and at some point there was no doubt that a certain amount of cash would have to be invested in the search. I decided to give Foster most of the information I possessed, but there did not seem any point in telling him about the photographs which had been sent to Barbara Haswell.

I poured out some wine. "Cheers! I promise not to drink three bottles or to dive out of the window."

Foster sipped his wine and said, "It's funny, but a lot of the time I was in Nissaki I had the impression that something strange was going on there. You remember that game Charades? Where you go out of the room and the others have to act something when you come back. Like that."

"Well one thing was going on—I'm fairly certain that Haswell and Reardon were diving for treasure. Having the room next to them I overheard them talking, and various things they said made me think they were. Then this morning I popped round to see Haswell's wife Barbara, and she described them both as being 'treasure mad'. I've got something upstairs to show you."

I went up to my bedroom and collected the papers I had carefully hidden. Returning to the kitchen, I felt that I ought to be vague about exactly when I had found the Phillips & Haswell letter-heading. I handed it to Foster, saying "I picked that up in the taverna."

Foster glanced at what was written on the page, then shot me a surprised look. I expected him to make some adverse comment on my tricky behaviour in keeping it. He may have made it mentally, but he said, "Lumke— Rennes—Poussin. Have you made anything out of this?"

"Not much. I've done a little research but only with negative results. There isn't a Peter Lumke in the London telephone book. Rennes is a largish town in France, on the River Vilaine. I can tell you what my dictionary of painters says about Poussin, but I don't think that is going to help us much."

"Perhaps not . . . it's hard to say." Foster's eyes glittered and I could see that he was intrigued by the enigmatic list. He was hooked on the treasure hunt, just as I had been. He muttered something, probably repeating a name on the list, then said, "May I make a copy of this? A good friend of mine, a professor at London University, has a brain like an encyclopaedia. He might come up with something."

"Go ahead. We can do with all the help we can get."

I watched him closely as he took out a small note-book and a tiny silver pencil: it's always interesting to see how other people tackle things. Foster's writing was precise, minute; he took his time in making an exact copy of every word apart from the printed heading, setting them out just as they were placed in the original.

When he had finished writing I said, "There's something else to go along with that. Like the bad fairy's curse. It came through my letter-box this morning."

Foster took the anonymous letter and raised his eyebrows. His otherwise impassive look remained as he read it, but he shook his head. He said slowly, "I don't think this is from a crank. I think Dave and Ken were close to finding something. Probably something very valuable. And these people. . . ." He shook the letter. "I think these people, Mr Townshend's friends—they exist. Well, all right, so let's see if we can find it. Are you on?"

"You bet."

"And what are the chances of Mr Townshend's friends stopping us?"

"I don't know."

"I do. Piss-poor."

14

An ALARMING AMOUNT of Bond Street is to let. Old-established firms like Herbert Johnson the hatters, Abdulla the cigarette shop and W. E. Hill the violin makers have disappeared, leaving blank, dark glass and typewritten notices about new premises. Other old firms have retreated to the country or quietly gone bankrupt. A rash of boutiques have sprouted and withered like weeds with poor roots. There has been some garish shop-fitting by European companies who regard sterling as little better than Monopoly money and are willing to lose some in order to gain a prestige address. Antique, labyrinthine premises have been replaced by those of steel and chrome design where a welcome is always combined with close appraisal. But it is the blank windows and the To Let signs which impinge on pedestrians with time to look for such things. Walking down from Oxford Street I had counted thirty-seven vacant premises when I reached that corner of Bond Street and Conduit Street known as "Bondstrasse". My concentration was broken by hearing my Christian name being called out in an incisive masculine voice from the Bruton Street corner. I turned to see the tall, spare figure of Alec Harvey who was signalling his intention of crossing over to join me. A rather enigmatic customer of mine with a nose for a bargain, Harvey was sometimes supercilious and taciturn, sometimes friendly. Intelligent, complex, I always found him interesting. A barrister who had retired at an early age with the reputation of having successfully defended the better class of criminal, he now appeared to be without an occupation. I could not think of a single business deal with him in which I had not suffered from the suspicion that he had got the best of it. He was the only man I knew who appeared to have improved his looks by going bald.

Waiting impatiently for the traffic lights to give him a chance to cross the road, Harvey gave out an aura of restless energy. As he came close his dark brown eyes looked greatly amused. "Well Harry, so you've returned at last! I thought you'd made so much money from those Russian leaflets that you'd retired to the sun for good. 'Sold to the man from the doll's house shop.' I bet you were furious."

"I wasn't pleased. Still, publicity of a kind I suppose. A surprising number of people seem to have noticed that small headline."

"I met the old man—Dolek Menkes—I met him at your shop once. You remember, you gave us an alfresco lunch. Smoked salmon, rye bread and Muscadet. What happened —how did he die?"

"Chronic bronchitis. He lived in a damp flat in Pimlico, the kind of place which should have been condemned. Bronchitis, pleurisy, pneumonia, finito." I contrived to give the impression that I had been in touch with Dolek to the end while skating round the fact that I had not visited him in hospital. Ah yes, I thought, I manage to let people down without other people getting to hear of it.

"Coffee?" Harvey suggested, inclining his Julius Caesar-like head in the general direction of Clifford Street.

"Coffee."

We walked along in silence. Harvey was the one person I knew most likely to tell me something about the late Victor Townshend. He had an unrivalled acquaintance-ship with all classes. He had a mill-house in Suffolk where his wife lived with their six children, but he also had a flat in Farm Street which I suspected was sometimes used for hanky-panky. At one of his Farm Street parties I had met several whizz-kid millionaires, London's best known bookmaker, suspect characters who looked as if they might have been Harvey's former clients, a Duke's eldest son, and the blonde actress I had hoped would write to me.

As we turned the corner into Clifford Street I felt reasonably certain that Harvey had some favour or request in mind for me; it had been indicated by his enthusiastic greeting and impatience at the traffic lights. And there was something else too in his manner, as something not quite genuine in a voice tells a wife that her husband is up to mischief, and I made a living partly by being sensitive to such things. There seemed to be a possibility of our swapping favours. Alec Harvey collected sixteenth-century poetry with the enthusiasm of a man who realises that he is on to a good thing, the knowledge of a specialist collector, and the cajolery of a dealer, but he occasionally asked my advice.

Once we were seated I decided to get my question in first, and I asked it hoping that a light tone might disguise my considerable interest in his reply. "Does the name Victor Townshend mean anything to you?"

He looked reflectively at me for a moment and I knew I was in luck.

"One of the Ormond Townshends, isn't he?"

"He was. He died in June."

"Ah, did he? Well, it's an ancient family name, Ormond Townshend, goes back beyond the Crusades, in which they were involved I believe. . . ." He broke off, struck by some thought.

"Has Master Sotheby got the wind of something coming on the market from their estate?"

"Not as far as I know. It's nothing to do with business. Just idle curiosity."

"I see, I see. Just idle curiosity." Harvey parroted my phrase in a tone of incredulity. "Well, I can tell you that it is a very rich family. They own, or owned, a sizeable slice of Wessex. . . ."

He paused again, perhaps weighing his words on the scales of caution. He reached for the sugar-bowl and took some time over taking a spoonful. "Something else, which might interest anyone with an idle curiosity about the family. They've always wanted to avoid publicity but seem to have attracted it somehow in backing away. What do they—there is a sister, or was—want to hide? That's been the Press's attitude. And I don't need to tell you, with the phrase 'doll's house' still ringing in your ears, that reporters can be very irritating sometimes. Ten to one there has never been anything to hide, they've just wanted to be left alone. A simple enough request, one which the papers are usually willing to afford to you and me."

"How rich?"

"Oh, extremely. No doubt that's what attracted the Press's attention in the first place. Wealth on that scale seems to have an obsessive fascination for journalists. Partly envy, of course. How rich?—well, not in the Ross Perrot or Daniel Ludwig class but. . . . There's a book by Daniel Lundberg called *Rich and Super Rich*—you could look them up in that."

"Anything else?"

Harvey gazed at me with eyes that were amused and slightly puzzled. "I always knew you for a persistent kind of chap, Harry, you have that reputation you know. But on behalf of idle curiosity?"

"Shall be humbly grateful for any scraps. I'll do my grovelling later."

"Will you? Good. There was a time, some years back, when the Townshend family might have said there was a mild kind of persecution campaign against them—by the popular Press. For a while photographs and accounts of their movements appeared regularly—the kind of publicity that pop-stars lap up. I remember seeing one photograph of Victor O. T., getting into a plane I think, turning round, looking just as indignant as Greta Garbo. Victimised by the camera, as it were."

"He died abroad. In Geneva."

"I see. That's probably the reason they've escaped publicity in recent years. In Switzerland the rich are left well alone, if that's what they want. But I dimly remember

83

one of the top papers over here running a story about their country estate, that the house had been closed and left to rot, or villagers protesting about a barred right of way, something like that."

"Many thanks."

"No need for thanks, old boy. Remember that slight price adjustment you felt you couldn't make on the Perry Shakespeare bust? I see you still have it in the window, gathering dust. There's a niche in my flat just made for it."

15

THE DOLEFUL TOLLING of a church bell turned into shriller ringing. The church bell sound turned out to be fiction, the end of a dream. The ringing was fact, the phone bell signalling the attention of an early, persistent caller. I glanced at my watch to see it was 6.25. American customers occasionally telephone at odd hours, having miscalculated the trans-Atlantic difference in time, and I got out of bed half expecting to hear an American accent. Instead there was a gruff Cockney voice.

"Mr Gilmour? Dainty Haswell wants to see you urgent."

The odd name struck an immediate chord, for the overheard phrase in Nissaki "We could do with dainty" still lingered in my memory, so I swallowed a comment about it being a strange time to phone and just queried the name.

"Yerss, Dainty Haswell. Look, he wants to see you straight'way. 'Bout his bruvver Dave. It's important, know what I mean. He says what about this mornin'?"

"Yes, okay. What time and where?"

"Up the Gate. Billingsgate. He says for you to wait inside the entrance, all right? The market entrance. Nine-firty?"

"I'll be there. How shall I know him?"

"Don't worry 'bout that, mate. You'll know him right enough."

The message ended on a slightly threatening note but I had the impression that this had become a habit with the caller rather than anything personal.

Another telephone conversation came in between shaving and breakfast. A slightly odd call that seemed to be coming from a long distance, punctuated by clicks and Munchkin voices, but was in fact from the airfield in Bucks where

Andrew Foster kept his Cessna aircraft. Andrew told me excitedly that he had traced the mysterious Peter Lumke whose name had been written on the paper I had picked up by the stone steps in Theo's Taverna. He said that Lumke was an art historian who lived in a remote part of Lincolnshire, and that he was going to fly there to see him. Andrew sounded much younger on the phone, like a schoolboy just setting off on a long awaited expedition. I told him that I had done a little investigating too, and that the Townshend family was so wealthy it seemed improbable that they would be interested in promoting or preventing treasure-hunts. "That's as may be," Andrew replied, "but I'm sure we're on to something. Tell you more, tell you why, when I've seen the elusive Lumke." The line went dead as if we had been cut off.

The third and in a way most surprising call came for me at 8.50, just when I was about to leave for Billingsgate Market. It too was heralded by some clicks. Then an attractive young female voice said, "Hello, you. Why haven't you phoned? You had the number." My pulse quickened absurdly, and for a moment I felt like a nervous love-sick youth, as I recognised it was Jane Mackmurdo. I said hello and then hesitated. She said, only half joking, "Don't say that this is the end."

It was true that we had swapped telephone numbers in saying goodbye at Heathrow, but I had thought this was a matter of form on her part; I had no more expected to hear from her again than the actress I had met at Harvey's party.

"I was biding my time. Waiting for an excuse."

"You fool! What made you think you needed one? I just wouldn't have given you the number. Anyway, would you like to come here and I'll play you some Chopin? I've got some rather good wine. I know you like wine. Remember?"

"Sounds wonderful. When?"

"This evening? May seem like rushing things but I'm

going away for a bit. The BBC job fell through. I'm feeling rather down about that. You must come and cheer me up."

"I'll try."

"Can you make it this evening?"

"It's a little difficult. I've got to motor to the Cotswolds this afternoon and collect some books. Can't really cancel that."

"Shall you be staying there overnight?"

"No, but I may be back rather late."

"That doesn't matter. Look, we agreed that Chopin went with moonlight, didn't we? I'll supply the Chopin, I'm not sure about the moon. You are allowed out at night I suppose?"

Her joky, faintly peevish manner was different from her cool approach in Corfu and I did not quite know what to make of it. She gave me her address in Spanish Place, adding, "I'm not a good cook, you'll find, but I shan't let you starve."

My mind was in a whirl after I had replaced the receiver, and I found it hard to concentrate when Mary Carpenter arrived wanting to ask me about various dull business matters. Instead of thinking about sending out statements to slow-paying customers, my mind was trying to deal with the various bits of information I had absorbed in the previous two hours. And I was as excited at the prospect of calling in at the Spanish Place flat as Andrew had been about flying to Lincolnshire. I dealt with Mary's questions hastily, said I had an early appointment in the City, reminded her I would be away after lunch, then ran out of the shop and down Duke Street to find a taxi.

A salty shrimp-like smell hit me as soon as I got out of the taxi by the Monument—like a whiff of the sea. A moment later I was properly immersed in a part of working London where men were trundling barrows, walking with fish-boxes piled on top of their padded bowlers, sluicing down shop-fronts, and backing lorries out of narrow alley-ways. As I went down the hill the fish smell became stronger and pervasive, the banter and back-chat continuous.

"I've got you-know-who on the trumpet."

"It's all shit or bust."

"He give me some GBH of the eardrum. He wants to knock 'em out a bit quick."

"He gets on my tits."

I had often seen the rear of Billingsgate Market from the Thames but I had never approached it directly. The number of men making their way to cafés and to the local pub, The Cock, made it obvious that the main business of the day was over, leaving only the clearing up to be done. I glanced up at the stone Britannia figure, supported by giant fish, on the top of the building, then walked in at the main entrance, picking my steps with care as the wet floor looked treacherous. There were rows of shop-like stalls at both sides of the high building, and offices overhead. Electric lights with grey metal shades hung down on very long leads. There was a series of signs with the names of firms. I stood under the first one by a row of empty barrows.

Within a minute I heard a tuneless whistle and turned to see a heavily built man in his late thirties coming in by another door. He was well over six feet in height, with over-wide shoulders that gave him a top-heavy look. He eyed me carefully, continuing to whistle an out-of-tune version of "Trees". I could just discern a likeness to Dave Haswell so I was in no doubt that I had recognised Dainty, as my caller had prophesied. This feeling became stronger as he approached me with a curiously light step, well up on his toes. It reminded me of a boxer with whom I had once fought an exhibition match, who had a similarly light step, a non-stop shuffling gait and an obtrusive thumb. Dainty had the same glossy dark hair and high colour as his brother, but could not be considered handsome as he had a large beaky nose that might appear either comical or threatening. His thick fingers looked like beef sausages and the knuckles were those of a one-time boxer, broken and set.

"Mr Gilmour?"

"Mr Haswell?"

We spent another minute looking each other over like the boxers we had once been. He could see that the angle of my nose had been adjusted from the direction Nature had intended; I noticed signs of stitching along his bony brows.

Our mutual inspection was interrupted by a small nervous-looking man who came in quickly through the main entrance and sidled up to Dainty, talking out of the side of his mouth.

"How's it going?"

"Quiet, very quiet. Nuffing much going on."

"Yes. Old Blacky wants to see you."

"I want to see him too. The prick."

The small man tugged at the lobe of his right ear, sniffed, and his tone became even more confidential, "I may be getting out, going on the knowledge, drive a cab."

Dainty shrugged his massive shoulders at this information but said nothing. After the small man had walked on towards the rear of the building Dainty smiled bleakly. "Granite," he whispered, touching his forehead. He coughed twice, trying to clear some persistent phlegm, and looked at me with faintly puzzled eyes. His manner was oddly courteous.

"Now what can I do for Mr Gilmour?"

"You asked me to come."

"That's right, that's right. But why? I'm so busy, sometimes I forget what's going on. Oh yes, now I remember. Young Barbara, she said you'd been round, talkin' about Dave."

"Yes, I didn't know him very well but I liked him—we were all sorry...."

Dainty held his head aslant. For a moment a different personality emerged, aggressive and threatening. He tapped his great swollen nose. "Fucking mystery that all right. That boy was a strong boy. Great swimmer. Now me, one length of the baths, that's me lot, but Dave. . . ."

"I know just how good a swimmer he was. He dived in one day to help me when I wasn't feeling too great, I'd had quite a bit to drink. Normally I'm quite a good swimmer so I know. . . . But if I'm right he may have been diving at that spot for treasure. A tricky business if there's only two of you. One gets tangled up in a wreck, something like that. . . ."

"Yerss, Barbara said you was on to that. Smart gal that. She reckoned you was thinking of trying to find the treasure yourself."

"Why not? If it really exists then why not try to find it? Wouldn't be such a waste then."

"You're right, mate. You see, young Dave, he always had this thing about treasure. The old man, he brought us up on his motter—you know, 'You never get somefing for nuffing'. Trouble was we never believed him."

Dainty paused, looking at me reflectively. "Say you did find somefing, all right it's ten to one against but just say you did, what about young Barbara?"

"She'd get a share. A share for Ken Reardon's family too. And there's going to be another partner, a Mr Foster who was out in Nissaki, he'll be in on it too."

"And one more partner, skip." Dainty tugged out a bulky wallet and extracted a much folded piece of paper, and handed it to me. It had the printed heading "Doubloons Ltd.", with the Praed Street address of Dave Haswell's flat. There were two type-written lines, signed D. Haswell, acknowledging receipt of £1,000 from G. Haswell "to be re-paid with 200% interest within three months". It was dated 1st August 1976.

"I told him. I said don't be silly, I don't need this. I mean, with bruvvers you don't do you? But he went on and on, said he couldn't pull it off without my grand but wanted it all proper, down on paper, strickly business like.

'Course he always was different to me. Now if someone round here—some clever cock—drops a ricket, I'll give him a right chi-hiking, know what I mean. I might lean on 'im a bit too. But Dave ... Well he was a strong boy, could have handled hisself, like you, but I don't think he'd had a punch-up since he left Roland Hill School, Tottenham."

Dainty sighed deeply and pulled a funny face. "Funny how things work out. I mean, him insisting on me having this receipt." He held out his large hand for me to shake. "So now there's five partners, all right?"

"Yes. Perhaps there's nothing, perhaps there is and we won't be able to get it, but if we do then a fifth share of something is better than nothing."

"Fair enough. Right. Then I shan't need this." Dainty tore up the paper and let the pieces fall on to the wet concrete floor. "Okay partner. Fancy a drink? Just 'cross the road."

"I wouldn't mind."

We left the building, which now seemed to be empty on the ground floor apart from a youth tidying a stall, and crossed Monument Street. As we came close to the entrance of The Cock, Dainty gestured at a printed notice in the window, saying, " 'Course this time of mornin' only us workers can get a beer."

"Tomato juice will do for me."

There was a jostling crowd in the public bar but a path opened through it for Dainty as if by magic. A pint of beer was automatically handed to him when we reached the bar. Dainty ordered my tomato juice, then stifled a prodigious yawn.

"Fair enough. I mean, one hand washes the other," he said thoughtfully. "Young Barbara. She doesn't miss a trick, you know. Anyfing you think of she's already thought it, still I'll see she goes right through Dave's stuff. 'Course she doesn't think anyfing'll come of it, I mean you can't blame her, Dave did have a right load of washouts. He thought he was goin' to get in on that Scillies treasure lark, got thrown out on his earhole. But this—this might be different. Certainly I never seed him so serious. Mind, he really needed the loot. You see, matter of two, three munfs ago he told me he'd put this uvver young tart, this Eileen, in the pudden club."

16

I DON'T KNOW for what psychological reason I decided to drive round to Spanish Place. Normally I avoid using my car for short journeys in London, preferring to walk, take a bus, taxi or tube. So why did I choose to drive the half mile or so that separates the Duke Street which joins Jermyn Street to the one that runs into Manchester Square? Certainly I was not under the illusion that Jane Mackmurdo was likely to be impressed by a four-year-old Lancia with fifty thousand miles on the clock and a dented wing. I imagined her having escorts of the kind you see driving round London in Mustangs, Porsches and brand new Bentley coupés, the inexplicably rich young men who crowd into expensive restaurants just before closing time. I would have struck a better note by arriving on a rusty bicycle wearing a sweat-shirt and tennis shoes. Possibly the explanation for my quirkish behaviour was quite simple—the miserable lack of self-confidence that had led to me cleaning my teeth three times before I set off for Spanish Place.

Parking my car round the corner in George Street, I still felt as hesitant as a bashful youth. Basically I had not got over my surprise at Jane actually phoning me to suggest a meeting. It was like longing to possess a Vermeer and then someone knocking on the door to deliver one.

For a few moments I stood on the corner of Spanish Place looking at the side of Hertford House, which faced the flats where Jane Mackmurdo lived, and then up at the stars. The heavy rain clouds which had obscured the sky all day during my trip to the Cotswolds had been blown away by a strong south-westerly wind and only a few small grey wisps were left, moving so quickly as to appear unreal and fanciful, like those in a stage setting. The front door at the address Jane had given me was open, so I entered and started to walk up the steps slowly. The elderly gait was not dictated by tiredness, though it had been a long day, but because I was trying to get into a more positive mood. Right, I thought, so all the physical attraction is on one side, well perhaps she likes father figures or has a yen for rather beat-up faces.

The door of the flat on the top floor was also open. I knocked on it and then pushed it a little wider. It led into a large hall with an unusually high ceiling and a faintly gloomy aspect. Light came from two old-fashioned standard lamps standing at each end of the hall but it was rather feeble. I heard a faint murmuring voice, knocked again and took two steps into the hall, then realised that Jane was standing at the far end of it with her back to me, engrossed in a telephone conversation. She was shaking her head vigorously and repeating the word "No".

She held the receiver a little away from her ear as if tempted to replace it on the stand, listening silently, then said, "Sick of it. Don't you understand? Why can't you understand that?"

I tiptoed backwards and waited in the doorway as she again listened in silence. After abruptly saying, "No, I won't," she replaced the receiver.

She stood quite still and her posture gave me an impression of dejection. I rat-tatted loudly on the door and called out, "Hello".

When Jane turned she gave me a mournful little smile and I could see she had been crying. She looked particularly lovely in a long blue and silver dress with tiny straps over her bare shoulders. I moved towards her rather hesitantly.

"I've come at the wrong time."

"No."

"Would you sooner I pushed off? Make it some other time?"

94

"Don't be silly. Stop talking."

She put her hands up on my shoulders and we kissed. There was a sweetness in her kiss, the strange magic between female and male that makes questions and explanations superfluous. After a few moments she put her head against my chest, clinging quite tight. I had noticed large tears on her cheeks and I watched one run down by her nose. She seemed adrift and forlorn. It was like comforting a frightened child and I held her lightly. She aroused protective feelings rather than sexual passion as she clung there, saying nothing. I noticed that the ornate wallpaper behind her was stained in one place where rain had come in through the ceiling, leaving a scar of bobbled plaster. The atmosphere of the hall was like so many places I had been in during my book-dealing career; once well-furnished dwellings which had seen better days and were going to seed, usually lived in by old people who could not cope with domestic work, where dusty rooms led to a squalid kitchen.

Jane stepped back but did not take her hands from my shoulders; she looked at me with a curious expression which made me think her feelings towards me were ambivalent. I knew you could experience a queer sort of enmity with someone you desired.

After this silent summing up she said, "A horrid thing...."

I thought an explanation of the tears was to be forthcoming but after a moment she added lamely, "The cork in the wine bottle—I couldn't get it out, I should have waited.... It's broken."

"I'm notorious for not being able to mend things but broken corks are different—those I can usually manage."

"Ah yes, you're strong. 'The quiet man with muscles'— that's how Hildegarde described you."

"Did she! I didn't think I'd registered with her at all."

"You can never tell about such things. But don't let it

95

go to your head. Nearly everyone in trousers made some kind of impression on her. I heard her say '*Verweile doch, du bist so schön*' once. About another man."

"A younger man?"

"Yes." She shook her head as if to indicate that enough had been said on that particular subject. "Do you mind tackling the bottle? I feel like lots of wine tonight, like you did in Sidari."

She led me through a badly lit passage-way, saying, "Don't let this place get you down. I inherited it absolutely intact from an aged great-aunt. She left me everything. I haven't got round to changing it at all yet. I cleared a wardrobe for my clothes, otherwise it's just as she left it. As you've no doubt noticed, it had all got too much for her at the end."

"Splendid high ceilings after Lilliput House. Some fresh paint and it'll look very attractive."

We passed through a large drawing-room, again lit inadequately by one standard-lamp. The curtains were not pulled and I could see the top of Hertford House silhouetted against the night sky. Jane gestured vaguely towards the window. "I couldn't run to a moon, but I ordered lots of stars."

The kitchen turned out to be not at all squalid. It was the only room in the flat with adequate lighting; a rather bare room containing only a Dutch dresser with shelves of crockery, one chair, a sink, an electric stove and an ancient refrigerator. There was a plate of sandwiches and a bottle of white wine on top of the refrigerator.

"Ah, an old-fashioned corkscrew," I said. "No problem there."

"I hope you like the wine. I asked a knowledgeable friend. He said it should be dry and similar to the one you enjoyed so much in Corfu."

I picked up the bottle. It was a Haut Poitou, from a good importer.

"Looks fine. I'm sure he's right." Instantly, absurdly, I felt rather jealous of her knowledgeable friend.

"Well, I'll leave you to it. I'll deal with the music department."

She turned on her heel. Perhaps she was being tactful in case after my boasting I should have a struggle with a recalcitrant cork, perhaps she just wanted to blow her nose and remove any trace of tears. I didn't object to being alone for a few minutes as my mind was in rather a whirl. It was strange being plunged into the world of a young girl again, particularly with one who appeared to be in an emotional tangle with another man. My position seemed to be a peculiar one, and rather tricky. I glanced at the cork and saw that it was not broken, just one of the narrow kind that does need a good tug. It had been well hammered in. I showed off to myself by extracting it with a steady, slow pull, saying, "With one bound Jack was free."

There was a loud burst of music, quickly turned down and then up again. I heard snatches of an old song: "Whooo . . . made me dream all day. . . . Whooo . . . is my happiness. . . . Whooo . . . made me answer yes. . . . Whooo . . . no one but you."

I thought: You've made an old man very happy. Jane had tried to guess my epoch of popular songs and had gone back to those of my parents' period.

After several weeks of unusually hot weather for England this was the first cool evening, and standing in the strange kitchen suddenly reminded me of my last visit to see Dolek, when I had made a pot of tea in his cluttered tiny scullery. It had been a bitterly cold day then and his flat was devoid of comfort. Lying in bed, a few days away from death, he had looked as if he had seen a ghost, his scanty hair awry and his face chalk-white. I shivered and poured myself a quarter glass of wine.

Immediately Jane called out, "I heard that. You're off to a good start. Fortunately there's another bottle in the fridge."

97

I drank the wine that was in my glass and carried the bottle, glasses and sandwiches through to the drawing-room. The standard lamp had been turned off, and the only light came from a large electric heater which was made to look like a coal fire with synthetic flickering flames. Jane had pushed a couch in front of the fire. She said, "I expect you find this place a bit weird. Of course I'm used to it, I've been coming here since I was about six. I can't remember anything ever changing. My aunt must have bought her wireless from Marconi or whoever. I know the whole flat needs decorating but at the moment I can't be bothered. . . ."

I poured out some wine and raised my glass, saying, "To Spanish Place".

"To us—to this evening. Hope the sandwiches will be all right. There's salmon and some salady ones with artichoke and mushrooms."

We sat down and began to eat and drink hungrily. My nervousness had fallen away. There seemed to be a rapport between us so that we could be silent together, like a married couple.

After a few minutes Jane peered at me closely. "You look tired. Was it the driving?"

"No, not the driving. But it was a slightly tricky situation. I was buying some books from a very nice old couple. I saw the books earlier this year but the old man was reluctant to part with them then. Now they need the cash for a new roof for their cottage. I found it a bit depressing. I see so many people like that, ending up."

"I suppose you would. But they're probably quite happy."

"I know. Anyway I'm feeling less tired and down every minute."

"That's good. I'm going to fetch that other bottle and load up my aunt's ancient radiogram with Fred Astaire 78s. We can have our Chopin later."

Walking round the couch she touched the back of my neck and sang:

> If with me you'd fondly stray
> Over the hills and far away

She was gone for quite a few minutes and the snatch of song lingered in my mind. It reminded me of another quotation from *The Beggar's Opera* that I had heard recently, and trying to track down who had said it teased my brain till she came back.

The sound of Astaire singing "Change Partners" preceded her return. She entered, looking amused.

"Very well then, Mr Gilmour. You won't be able to say you can't dance to that."

"I thought your generation didn't do that old-hat kind of dancing."

"I'm not a generation. I'm me. Come on."

I took her in my arms and she whispered something I could not catch. I said "What?" and she said "Kiss me, you fool." After that kiss I caught my breath. Strange to describe the warmth of her embrace as being like wading into bitterly cold water, but it was as much of a surprise as that for me.

*   *   *

I awoke from a dreamless sleep and knew instantly where I was even though the first thing I saw was pale, wavering light in a strange oval mirror. Stars filled a tall window. Jane's arm was flung across my chest and her head was half on my pillow. I turned my head towards her and breathed in the sweet breath coming from her nose. I stared at her intently as if close scrutiny would enable me to understand her. Her love-making had been exciting but nearly claustrophobic in its intensity. It was as if she had some secret motive. I was not foolish enough to think that she had found the first encounter with me sufficiently exciting to be so carried away. Was she trying to punish her other lover?

For several minutes I watched the shifting silver and grey in the dressing-table mirror, trying to understand Miss Jane Mackmurdo, then got out of bed, detaching her arm very gently and moving in slow motion so as not to disturb her. The sky was cloudless, brilliant with stars, and from the window I had an oblique view of part of St James's Church in George Street, looking suitably mysterious at night. I was struck by what odd places churches are, where people congregate, trying to understand the inexplicable.

"Come back. Who gave you permission . . . ?" It was a jokey kind of question but Jane's voice was quite serious. As I padded back towards the bed there were several questions I wanted to ask her but couldn't. In particular, I wanted to say : What is this about? I'm middle-aged and no longer think I'm the cat's whiskers. Do you really care a scrap for me, or am I just tit-for-tat for that man who was phoning when I arrived?

I said nothing and she whispered, "Stand there a moment. At night one is what one should be. This is you, the real, the natural you."

I shivered and she said, "All right. You didn't need to do that. You can get back in now."

"You're a funny girl."

"No I'm not. Not now anyway. If you had seen me when I went for that BBC interview, met me in the lift there, I'd have been funny then all right. But not now."

I took her in my arms again and she lay silent, and I thought perhaps there is no catch and she does mean it. I felt reproved. A dangerous activity, I thought, such passionate love-making, where nothing is held back, because the heart is sure to be moved by it and I shall feel bound up with this girl whom I don't understand at all.

She lay with her head against my chest, so still that I was not sure whether she was sleeping or not, and I began to get cramp in my arm. Suddenly she said brokenly, "Treacherous . . . can't stand it any more . . . want the truth."

It seemed as if some bottled-up complaints were about to emerge and I waited, aware of the irony of my position, knowing that I was hopelessly placed to criticise any other man who had been having an affair with her. Silence lengthened between us and I asked, "What do you mean?"

She sighed deeply and twisted about in my arms as if to express her inability to say more.

Our closeness, and a liking for pillow-talk when one says things that are normally not spoken, made me want to confide in her, and I began to tell her how it looked as if I might get involved in the treasure-hunt which had obsessed Dave Haswell. She listened in silence for a while, but when I said it seemed likely that Haswell and Reardon had drowned in an attempt to find something off Karagol Point she said, "No, I don't believe that. I don't think there is any treasure waiting to be picked up at Kouloura. I heard that awful man Morley discussing the idea with Theo. Theo positively hooted at the suggestion. I mean, he would know if any ships had been sunk there. I should forget it."

I did not want to involve her with the letter that had warned me about Townshend's demented friends so I shrugged and let the matter drop. We were comfortably entwined and after a few more minutes I could tell from a change in her breathing that she had fallen asleep. I soon followed suit.

17

Lᴉʟʟɪᴘᴜᴛ Hᴏᴜꜱᴇ. Saturday, 2nd October 1976.

Mary Carpenter closed the shop and left at twelve-thirty for a weekend in Guildford, but I spent all the day working. I tried hard to concentrate on piffling activities, like checking overdue accounts and deciding to whom to send statements, but my memories of those eight hours pieced together would not fill five minutes.

At about six o'clock I went for a walk round St James's Park and the Palace Gardens. I had done that circuit so often that I hardly took in anything I saw apart from the fortified palace walls which reminded me fleetingly of the remote house at Aghios Stephanos. My mind was obsessed with Jane Mackmurdo; indeed, at one point I said "uncontrollably on the brain" out loud.

I was remembering the strange looks she had given me after our night of love-making. She had looked at me as a pregnant girl might do at a lover she thought would let her down when he learned the truth. Half a dozen times she had seemed to be on the point of saying something—just as many times I had choked back the question "What's wrong?"

Was she upset about something I did not comprehend? Or just disillusioned at seeing me as I really was, in the unromantic light of early morning, a middle-aged man hunting for his socks? She had seemed remote over our shared coffee and toast, and when we had said goodbye her assurance that she would contact me again in a few days time had been given half-heartedly, like someone administering a placebo. Thinking about Miss Mackmurdo got me nowhere. I doubted my capacity ever to understand what made her tick, and by the time I reached Mason's

Yard again I had decided to have an early supper and go to a cinema just in order to stop brooding on her.

My cat Magoo was waiting on the stairs when I entered Lilliput House, and made it obvious that he would welcome having his evening meal earlier for a change. I had just got out a tin of food for him when the door-bell rang. It was too late to be a customer and for a moment I felt sure it was Jane calling—to blurt out an explanation of her strange behaviour. Excitement, pleasurable anticipation, mystification, guilt—impossible to list all the different feelings I experienced as I hurried downstairs. But halfway down I was struck by the thought that it was equally possible to be Dorothy, having decided to cut short her stay in Hamburg. In a second my mind shaped the fantasy of opening the door and being confronted by both Dorothy and Jane: my wife who had every virtue except youth and sexual passion; the surprisingly passionate girl I found so enigmatic.

Instead of a feminine face I saw Andrew Foster's, looking strangely grubby as though made up for a tramp's role in amateur theatricals. His eyes were tired and bloodshot, and there were grease marks on his face, one of them appearing like a third eyebrow.

"Hope it's not very inconvenient, Harry. Thought you would want to know right away. I'm sure I've found out what young Dave and Ken were after."

"Really! That's great. Come in and have a drink."

"What I'd like. I know exactly what I'd like. Been flying and travelling all day. Fiddling with an oil-leak, then I buzzed up to London on a moped I carry in the Cessna. First I'd like a good wash. Then I could drain a teapot."

"That can be arranged. Bathroom's up one flight, door on the left. I'll make some tea."

Magoo had retreated to the kitchen window on hearing Foster's voice and his loud tread on the stairs. I put out some meat for the cat and then laid the table with a wholemeal loaf, butter, cheddar cheese, tomatoes and spring onions. I made some tea and poured myself a Guinness.

Foster appeared looking as if he had washed away his weariness along with the grease. "That's better. First things first." He drank a cup of tea and immediately poured another one, then began to make an enormous sandwich. When this was completed he regarded it with satisfaction, pulled out a small notebook and waved it at me. "All in here. The mystery of Rennes-le-Château. Remember the name Rennes was on the list you found in the taverna? Well, it's not the city but a tiny village called Rennes-le-Château. Perched on a hill-top to the south of Carcassonne, on the way to the Spanish border. Everything on that list fits together and makes sense. The name Lumke for instance —and Poussin. I told you Peter Lumke is an art historian —well, he's also an expert on Poussin. I flew to Lincoln to see Lumke but he's touring in France at the moment. However, I saw his wife . . . half a minute." Foster began to eat his sandwich with the relish of someone really hungry.

Watching Andrew, I was busy revising the opinion I had of him. In Corfu he had often seemed rather lost and out of place, a slightly eccentric figure, wandering about aimlessly with his map and binoculars. Now he had revealed himself as someone much more capable and practical than myself, making sense out of that disjointed list and tracking down Lumke, tackling everything with as much gusto as he had for this makeshift meal.

"Lumke's wife Mary. She was shaken rigid when I told her those lads had been drowned. Apparently Dave Haswell was on the phone to her husband only a mouth ago, asking some more questions. And those two definitely went to Rennes. Yes, it all fits together like a watch, but you'll have to read this. If I try to tell it you'll get confused; it will all be jumbled up. I think I've got the story down fairly straight on paper but you'll need to read it quietly. . . ."

I was impatient to start reading but Foster had replaced

the notebook in his pocket. It was obvious that his plan of campaign even included a notion of how to deal with me. He paused halfway through making another sandwich, saying: "Mrs Lumke was interesting. I could tell she didn't know a great deal about this business. I mean, she immediately put her hand on two relevant articles her husband had written, but she's never been to Rennes herself. Still, I could feel a woman's intuition at work. You know that queer way they solve a problem without knowing how it's been done. She seemed nervous."

"Because of her husband? Is he hunting for the treasure too?"

"No. Not a chance. According to Mary Lumke he's not remotely interested in it. . . . He only comes in because he's an authority on Poussin, and a Poussin painting is right at the centre of the mystery. You'll see. . . . Well, you read my notes tonight and decide if you want to go to Rennes. I could fly us there tomorrow."

"Hold on a minute. You mean fly there in your plane?"

"Perfectly safe, old man. Don't like blowing my own trumpet, but I'm reckoned a fairly good pilot."

"I'm sure. Just taken me a bit by surprise—the idea of flying to Rennes—like that."

"Flying to Carcassonne. That's the nearest airfield. Then we'd have to hire a car. The flight would take up all the daylight hours tomorrow. We would actually get to Rennes on Monday. What do you think?"

"I could get away for two or three days. That's no problem."

"Well, you brood on it after you've read my notes. If you're keen we'll meet at Booker airfield tomorrow at about ten a.m. If you don't want to try it, just give me an early call in the morning."

Foster had already stirred up enough keenness in me so that I felt like agreeing to his plan; but first I thought I should tell him of my own faltering progress towards solving the mystery, in which I had seemed to take two steps forward and three steps back. I told him I had committed us to sharing the treasure, if we ever found it, with the relatives of Dave Haswell and Ken Reardon, but he just nodded amiably at this, commenting, "Fair enough. We should do that." Then I admitted to an indiscretion in having mentioned the matter to Jane Mackmurdo. Foster grinned slightly at this confession and said, "I thought you two were getting on well. This'll surprise you. I popped round to see her at that rather posh flat in Spanish Place. Just to return a guide book on Corfu she lent me in Nissaki. She's a very nice girl."

After Foster had passed lightly over these matters which had been worrying me slightly, I told him that I had found out some information regarding the Townshend family; but as I started to recount the meagre facts I had got from Alec Harvey, he began nodding away again and said, "Sorry to be such a know-all, Harry, but I got quite a dossier on the Townshends from a friend of a friend who works in Fleet Street. In fact I've even seen an aerial photo of their house called Old Court in Dorset. It seems that most of the publicity they've attracted over the years has been to do with the hamlet, Toller Parva, which they own. The church there was burned down early in the 1920s. Then they let the cottages become derelict. Now, apparently, the house is boarded up and becoming derelict too."

"I can't see how there can be a connection between Dorset landowners and two Cockney treasure-hunters."

"Nor do I. Perhaps there isn't. Let's face it—anonymous letters are often written by someone with a screw loose. But the mystery of Rennes-le-Château has definitely got me hooked. It will be interesting to see if it has the same effect on you."

18

The Mystery of Rennes-le-Chateau

In 1885 a young priest named Bérenger Saunière was sent to Rennes-le-Château, a hill-top village which overlooks the valley of the River Aude. Saunière's early years in such a remote, small village may have seemed like a period of exile for an intelligent ambitious man; it was certainly a time of poverty for him during which he could not afford even humble lodgings and lived by himself in a tumble-down cottage. The village church was also dilapidated, but in 1891 Saunière managed to raise sufficient funds to begin some essential repairs. He had the damaged altar-stone lifted up and discovered that the supporting pillars were hollow and that one of them contained some old documents. There were passages from the Gospels but also some messages in code.

Saunière must have realised that the ciphers would have to be studied by an expert and he borrowed some money in order to go to Paris. There he consulted the Director of Saint Sulpice Church who arranged for a palaeographer to examine the coded passages. After a few days, during which Saunière began a friendship with the opera star Emma Calvé, he was given the results of the expert's decoding. Saunière then went to the Louvre where he bought a copy of Poussin's painting *Les Bergers d'Arcadie*, "The Shepherds of Arcadia". In this enigmatic work, believed to have been painted in Rome about 1640, a shepherdess and three shepherds are shown studying a tomb with the inscription *Et in Arcadia ego*, "Even in Arcadia, I, Death, am present".

When Saunière returned to Rennes-le-Château his mode

of living changed dramatically. He bought land and built a large house, the Villa Bethanie—the house is out of proportion to others in the village and overshadows the church. He also had a stone tower, the Tour Magdala, constructed at the very edge of the hill, just beyond his house. No one seems to know the purpose of the tower as similar views of the valley are to be had from the top floor of the Villa Bethanie. He spent large sums of money in having the church restored and decorated in a bizarre style. The paintings he had made for it all seem to have some special significance, as if Saunière was himself attempting to leave another coded message. Close to the entrance of the church he installed a large effigy of the Devil. Most strange of all, Saunière placed this inscription above the church door: *Terribilis est Locus Iste*, "This place is terrible". It is said that the Bishop who came to bless the restored building was so disturbed by the decorations that he paid no more pastoral visits.

There seems no doubt that Saunière's wealth was connected with secrets he had unravelled with the decoding of the messages. He took various steps to protect these secrets: he moved some of the stones in the churchyard and obliterated inscriptions, notably one on the grave of Marie de Negri d'Ables, Countess of Blanchefort. This had been prepared in 1781 by the Blanchefort family chaplain, Antoine Bigou, reputed to have been the author of the manuscripts hidden in the altar. However, it is still possible to study this inscription as it had earlier been copied by a collector of such things and reproduced in a book of churchyard inscriptions. At first sight this odd epitaph too seems to be in code, but part of it is simply the Latin phrase written in the Greek alphabet: *Et in Arcadia ego.*

What treasure could Saunière have discovered? This is an area where the Nazis are said to have carried out excavations during the war: it is now forbidden to treasure-hunters and amateur archaeologists, littered with the signs *Fouilles Interdites*, "Digging Forbidden". It is also the site of Aerada, one time fortified citadel of the Visigoths who in A.D. 410 sacked Rome. The historian Procopius tells us that their booty included : "... the treasures of Solomon, King of the Hebrews, a sight most worthy to be seen...." In A.D. 679 Dagobert, the King of the Merovingians, was assassinated. It is believed that his son Sigebert was taken to Aerada, assumed the title of Count of Razes, and eventually was buried in Rennes. One of the messages which Saunière found contains the significant phrase : A DAGOBERT IL ROI ET A SION EST SA TRESOR, ET IL EST MORT, "This treasure belongs to King Dagobert and to Sion, and he is dead". The word "Sion" (Jerusalem) is to be found in other inscriptions, and appears to be of crucial significance.

Shortly before a fatal stroke in January 1917 Saunière had signed a contract for further building works which would have cost some million francs. But at the reading of his Will a few weeks later it was shown that in fact Saunière owned nothing—his houses, land and other belongings were in the name of his housekeeper Marie Denarnaud. It is reputed that Saunière made a confession on his deathbed and that the priest who heard it was deeply upset. Saunière's housekeeper lived on in comfort till her death in 1953. She had promised to pass on "a secret" before she died, but at the end of her life she was paralysed and left speechless by a cerebral haemorrhage.

Only two of the parchments which Saunière found have survived but one of them includes the intriguing message, in a very complicated cipher, "Poussin holds the key!" When a reproduction of the Louvre painting (Nicolas Poussin's second treatment of this theme : an earlier, quite different one is in the Duke of Devonshire's Chatsworth collection) is studied the connection can be seen. The tomb is one at Arques only a few miles from Saunière's church, and in the background are the remains of the Château of Blanchefort and the hill of Rennes-le-Château. Another mysterious link is a letter written by Poussin's brother to

Nicolas Fouquet who was Superintendent of Finance in the court of Louis XIVth. This letter, which has always puzzled art historians, was dated the 17th April 1656. Part of the letter is as follows:

He and I discussed certain things, which I shall with ease be able to explain to you in detail, things which will give you, through M. Poussin, advantages which even Kings would have great pains to draw from him and which according to him it is possible that nobody else will ever rediscover in the centuries to come. . . .

So it seems that Poussin knew of an extraordinary secret, that he used the background of Rennes-le-Château for his strange painting *Et in Arcadia ego*; and it was this very work, reproduced in stone, which Poussin chose to decorate his own tomb in Paris.

19

A PLEASANTLY RELAXED atmosphere at Booker Airfield : arriving there was like driving into a tennis club.
There seemed to be no signs prohibiting parking, walking
on the grass or indeed anything else. At first, going on my
long and tedious experience of commercial airports, I was
puzzled by this, and then I realised that amateur pilots fly
partly for the sense of freedom it gives them and like to
avoid all but essential rules.

I parked my car, locked it, and stood, holding my overnight bag, looking round with pleasure at the brightly
coloured aircraft and the clear blue sky. It was a perfect
autumn day : there had been a mist on the road out of
London but the sun had seen it off and produced a shirt-
sleeve temperature without humidity that was just right
for me. Walking away from the Lancia I realised that I
had forgotten my Michelin Luchon-Perpignan map which
I had told Foster I would bring. Typical of me, I thought;
like my unzipped fly at Dolek's funeral.

To say that I was apprehensive when I spied Andrew's
Cessna would be a crude way of expressing a far from
simple equation. After seeing several impressive looking
two-engined aircraft, I suddenly spotted Andrew standing
by a relatively tiny beige and cream coloured plane which
was being filled up with fuel. Andrew had a possessive
hand laid on its body as if it was a horse; he was chatting
away to a mechanic dressed in white overalls, and the re-
fuelling seemed as informal a matter as having petrol put
into a car. And indeed the Cessna appeared to be not much
larger than a Mini with a wing tacked on to it. The idea
of flying to a place near the Spanish border in such a small
machine appeared absurd. But my suspect willingness to

drop business at the least excuse and fly away on a wild
goose chase, searching for dubious treasure, also entered
into my reactions. I remembered the comments that were
endlessly repeated in my school reports: "Must concentrate", "Lacks perseverance", "Must try harder". How
prophetic they had been!

Instead of walking across to the Cessna, I remained in
the shadow of a magnificent large white aircraft. Guilt
because of my fecklessness prompted me to pull out a letter
from Dorothy which the postman had handed to me just
as I was leaving Lilliput House. The letter was very like
her, affectionate but a little detached, written with quiet
wry humour:

> Much enjoying Hamburg because of dear J and despite
> the city which is all too 21st Century for me. J's friends
> are super-intelligent scientist types. Stimulating in small
> doses but I begin to flag. . . . J said she was "rather
> worried" that you and I "seem to be moving further
> apart". I said that all relationships are usually both
> better and worse than they appear from the outside, and
> if we do move apart we also move closer from time to
> time, which is very nice. Can't face the prospect of
> another city immediately after futuristic Hamburg but
> hope. . . .

Hearing my name called out by Andrew, I stuffed the
letter into my pocket. His voice carried me back to the
holiday in Nissaki, and I half expected him to come stumping over with bad news about the water shortage at the
taverna. Instead he gave a brief wave and seemed to study
me closely as I walked across the grass. I realised our roles
had been reversed. In Nissaki I had been the sun-and-sea
worshipper, very much at home, while he limped across
the stones bearing bad tidings. At Booker he was in his own
element while I felt rather lost. He was wearing a navy

wind-cheater and dark glasses which changed his appearance to a surprising extent, deleting the slightly old-fashioned impression.

"Hello, Harry! Meet the Skylark. A Cessna 175. Golf-Alpha-Romeo-Foxtrot-Golf," he said, tapping the large initials on the body of the plane. "You'll be hearing that call-sign till you're sick of it during the next couple of days. Fortunately for us English is the international air language. How's your French by the way?"

"Poor. Schoolboy level and what I learnt off the side of the sauce bottle: '*Le sauce HP est un mélange de qualité de fruits orientaux*'."

Andrew took off his glasses and grinned for a moment at my joke. "Mine's not bad. I've done quite a bit of flying there and they only speak English strictly while you're in the air. The moment you touch down they want you to parlez in a more civilised tongue."

The re-fuelling was completed and Andrew turned away to say something to the mechanic. I was mentally reviewing the crew of the Cessna 175. Pilot, navigator, wireless operator, linguist and man of the world: A. Foster. Supercargo: H. Gilmour.

He turned back asking, "And how's your bladder control?"

"Nothing special."

"Well the gents is over there. You won't be surprised to hear that there is no lavatoire aboard the Skylark. The first hop, to Hurn, is only about fifty minutes, but flying does sometimes seem to affect the old water-works."

"No, I'll be all right."

Andrew nodded and took my bag to place it in the Cessna. "So—you were hooked by the mystery of Rennes."

"I'm curious certainly."

"Some reservations?"

"Let's put it this way. I'm keen to go there, and *very* keen to see that church. Intrigued by that all right. But the story of Bérenger Saunière and his treasure—that doesn't make sense to me."

"How do you mean? Perhaps it's my fault. Don't forget, you were reading notes I fudged up from Professor Lumke's articles. Perhaps I made a hash of it."

"No, it's not that. It's the basic idea. I mean, if Saunière did find some treasure, then what was so worrying about it that the priest who came to see him was frightened by his deathbed confession? And what can be the connection between treasure and the inscription over the church 'This place is terrible'. If Saunière found treasure and was able to use it to re-build the church, surely that would have been good?"

"True. Frankly I didn't worry too much about the logic of it all. Just found it fascinating and wanted to know more. And the only way to do that is to go there, right? I don't know about you but places, things—they're not real for me till I've seen them. When I've actually touched that Devil inside the church door, when I've read that inscription, then possibly it'll make more sense."

"I agree about that. And I'm not having second thoughts about going. Just puzzled that Peter Lumke didn't dig deeper, he seems to have simply plonked down facts without getting any pattern."

"Yes, but basically he was only interested in the Poussin angle. There's much more to that side of it, but I didn't want to make the story too complicated."

Andrew walked to the tail of the plane and then round it, obviously checking on various points. "Well, we're off then. You're not worried about the flight, old man? Piece of cake really. I can land this little bird on a cricket pitch, you know. And they didn't call me the survivor of Tangmere for nothing."

His last sentence was rather less reassuring than he intended. I linked the word survivor more with someone who walks away from wrecks than a good pilot. I remembered that the R.A.F. had a club for the airmen who had come down in the sea and survived. When Andrew turned to face me again my eyes flicked over his jacket to see if there was a small significant badge pinned to it.

"In we get then. You're on the right."

Confidence in Andrew's ability as a pilot returned as soon as he began to taxi the Cessna across the field. I could see it was no more to him than my getting the Lancia out into Duke Street. He began to mumble something, and I realised he was not talking to me but to the control-tower requesting permission to take off. It was odd sitting behind the duplicate set of controls without having any idea how to use them. Probably nerves made me see the funny side of things and imagine working at them at the same time as Andrew with disastrous results. He said something else into the radio and revved up the engine; for a few moments the small plane throbbed in a stationary position, and then we took off. The ascent was so quick and was made to appear so easy that I realised I was in the hands of an expert and stopped worrying about the dangers of the flight. I could see how well equipped Andrew was for the job, with his 20–20 vision, his obsession with maps, and an all-essential calmness, an ability not to worry if things went wrong.

The take-off petered out just before a road and I looked down to see the shadow of our plane crossing it like a flying beetle. We made a leisurely turn till we were pointing south and could see the Thames meandering across our flight path. Andrew spoke confidentially into the radio once more, then turned to me. His raised voice sounded tinny and nasal. "Next stop Hurn. We go through customs there and I have to file a flight plan, a V.F.R. to cross the Channel. Then we hop across to Cherbourg. Have to report there—time for a sandwich. *Et puis*, with any luck at all, all the way with LBJ. I mean, non-stop to Carcassonne. That will certainly take bladder control so I advise only one drink and no coffee, okay?"

I nodded, finding it hard to concentrate on conversation with so much to look at. Nothing like a bird's-eye view for giving one a sense of proportion. How unimportant our tiny shadow appeared as it crossed fields in which the grass had been burned brown by months of sun! I was struck by the patterns to be seen from that height, the order and geometric lay-out of streets. The fields looked much too neat to be real, and a farm with a tractor chugging along a dusty track seemed just like a toy one set out by a child.

A bulky map, complicated with red lines and symbols, was jammed into a thin black brief-case by Andrew's feet, but he did not refer to it on the flight to Hurn. We flew so steadily that after a while it was like being in a bus. Andrew looked down at a town and checked his watch. A moment after he turned as if to say something but changed his mind.

For a while he fiddled with a circular sliderule whilst appearing mentally to debate whether to raise a point with me. He was faster on his mental feet than I had thought, but I had one advantage over him: twenty years of dealing with people in business had given me a great deal of experience in knowing how they react, seeing through feigned disinterest, sensing reluctance. Eventually he said, "The point I'd expected you to raise. . . . What I thought you'd query was what can possibly be the link between Rennes-le-Château and treasure-hunting off Karagol Point?"

"That's a puzzle all right but not one I expected we could solve easily. If Mrs Lumke is right about those recent telephone calls from Dave Haswell there may well be some connection. And going to Rennes there's just a chance we can find it."

"Yep, I mean, there's a whole lot of puzzling stuff but what have we got? Haswell and Reardon went to Rennes —fact. Haswell made several phone calls to Professor Lumke about Rennes—fact. Then Haswell and Reardon turned up in Nissaki with all their underwater equipment—

fact. Snakes and ladders progress, old man—that's all we can hope for. A lucky throw that puts us on the ladder leading from Rennes to Corfu."

*   *   *

Hazy sunlight as we approached the Channel and then unimpeded glare of sun over it. I began to sweat as we struggled into ancient looking yellow life jackets. Andrew fussed over me as we did this, pointing out the whistle and the hand-inflator to be used if the automatic one failed.

Struggling to keep awake flying over the Channel—strong soporific effect of flying through the sunlight reflected by the sea—losing hold—like strange fleeting moments in the dentist's chair while waiting for an injection to take effect, staring at the bright blank sky with the mind becoming detached, remote. . . .

*   *   *

Perfunctory customs inspection at Cherbourg. Three clocks in the flight control office all showed different times and none of them agreed with my watch. Odd conversation between Andrew and one of the officials about time, none of which I could understand, even when part of it was in English. "Zulu" time appeared to be crucial. What the hell is "Zulu" time I thought but did not ask, not wishing to underline any more inadequacies as a member of the expedition. At one moment both Andrew and the French official appeared nonplussed by the complications of "Zulu" time. Simultaneously they pulled funny expressions like those actors in Tarzan films had when they weren't sure what emotion they should be conveying.

*   *   *

"Hey-up! Wakey-wakey!" Andrew's insistent voice woke

me up from a disturbing dream in which I had followed Jane Mackmurdo and some other people I did not recognise, first through a churchyard and then into a church. I had pursued Jane persistently though she had made it plain that she wanted to escape my attentions. We had squeezed past the end of a pew, through a door into a dark passage-way, and then had started to mount a corkscrew staircase. There were tantalising glimpses of Jane's legs as we went up the winding stairs. At one point I had touched her ankle and she had said "No". I had replied in a smart-alec way, "When the lady says no does she really mean yes?". A moment later the feminine figure with shapely legs had stopped and my hand slipped up to her knee. Then a strange voice had murmured "What is it you want?" and a face had looked down into mine. But instead of Jane it was Marianne Prothero's plump face, her eyes glittering darkly and her sensual mouth pouting.

"Good! Glad you managed to wake up. Funny, but I always like to have my passengers *compos mentis* when I land. I know I'm good but I'm not that good. That's the airport below, and the city of Carcassonne to the left. God, they've tarted it up with all those lights!"

Below I could see the ramparts of the ancient walled city illuminated by a glow of red lights. Dropping down to a remote airport in the twilight made an exciting start to our quest for the treasure, but my mind was still going over the events of my dream as Andrew turned to line up the Cessna for landing. I probed the last moments of the dream, trying to match the voice asking "What is it you want?" with my vague memory of how Mrs Prothero had talked. Something about the voice was wrong and it puzzled me; it was as if the answer to the teasing question was just round a corner in my brain but unwilling to emerge.

20

THE BUSINESS OF hiring a car turned out to be a more complicated and protracted affair than we expected. After an excellent breakfast at the Hotel du Pont Vieux I thought we would be driving away from Carcassonne within half an hour, but Monsieur Ducret, the car firm's young representative, had different ideas. We waited over two hours for him to arrive, and when he did it was plain that he had a passion for bureaucratic procedure. He examined my driving licence minutely as if anxious to discover that it was a forgery, then insisted on us inspecting the old but highly polished Citroën at length, verifying that there was a spare tyre and a complete tool kit and that the tyres were all in good condition. Afterwards he sat down in the hotel lounge and pulled out a mass of forms to be completed in duplicate.

My short fuse began to fizz, and after mutely communicating with Andrew I got up and left him to deal with the formalities before I developed a bad attack of Francophobia.

There was a milky-grey dull sky but it was good to get out into the street and escape the fumes of Ducret's Gauloise. Our hotel was about halfway between the busy modern section of Carcassonne and the ancient walled city perched right at the top of the hill. I walked up and down, impatient to be off, thinking about the odd trail that had led me to being outside the Hotel du Pont Vieux—the phrases overheard in Theo's Taverna, Haswell's enigmatic notes and the anonymous letter with its warning about "the demented friends of the late Mr Townshend".

I looked at my watch to see that it was twelve-forty. So much for our planned departure at ten o'clock. A moment later Monsieur Ducret appeared, first waving his brief-case to signal a satisfactory termination of difficult negotiations, then approaching to shake my hand and wish me good luck. He was brimming over with Gallic charm, flashing his teeth and offering me a Gauloise, and my pangs of Francophobia vanished.

Andrew and I were in the Citroën within seconds of Ducret's departure. The car interior smelt of Gauloises and musky perfume but somehow that did not seem objectionable, just part of being in France. It took me a few minutes to find the way out of the city, driving west and then south on to the N118. Once we were on the main route running south, following the course of the River Aude, I re-discovered how pleasant it could be to drive on a good road with relatively little traffic.

We stopped briefly in Limoux to buy a picnic lunch so that our time in Rennes-le-Château could be spent without bothering about a meal : a loaf, cheese, two slices of ham, a handful of olives in a screw of brown paper and a bottle of local wine in an unlabelled bottle. A riverside meadow just beyond the ancient village of Alet-les-Bains proved to be a perfect site for an alfresco meal. Andrew had bought a Michelin map in Carcassonne and he examined it while I uncorked the wine. He showed that Rennes-le-Château was marked with a star-like symbol that denoted a "Panorama". While we ate he outlined a plan of campaign : that I should prowl round the church and churchyard, taking photographs of anything that struck me as interesting, while he would search out a woman in the village who—according to Mrs Lumke—possessed some magazines with articles about Bérenger Saunière. As his French was fluent and mine was poor this seemed a sensible division of labour.

At Couza we took a left turn and almost immediately the road began to twist and climb up from the valley. Andrew's attention was concentrated on the Michelin map. He moved his stubby fore-finger along the N613 road to Coustaussa and Arques, making calculations and mumbling to himself.

Agnostic, sceptic, allergic to anything to do with the supernatural, why did I experience some strange sensation as I drove the old Citroën up the steeply twisting road to Rennes-le-Château? Certainly it was not mounting excitement at actually being within a mile of the possible source of treasure for I had never had much hope of us making a discovery of that kind. Had I been so brainwashed by the odd story of Saunière that when I saw the hill where he had lived my imagination responded immediately? The feeling I had contained some indefinable oppressive element; it was so strong that I felt that Andrew must also sense this melancholy undertow and glanced at him, but he was still absorbed in the map.

He looked up as we entered the village, clapped his hands together and said, "Well, we made it! It's no good —before I find that Madame Brichot with the magazines I must see the church. Okay?"

The streets were very narrow and not intended for cars. I parked the Citroën by a parapet where there was a dramatic view of the valley and we continued further up the hill on foot. The village appeared deserted and all the windows were closed or shuttered. We saw no one and the only sounds we heard were of a dog barking and a cock crowing.

The exterior of the church looked as if it was again in need of repair: slates were broken in the roof and the tower looked decrepit. We walked through a small circular garden at the front and stared up at the inscriptions above the stout wooden door. There were several in Latin of a conventional kind but the one Andrew had been so keen to see was also there, in a central position: TERRIBILIS EST LOCUS ISTE.

I noticed that there was the date 1891 on a stone pillar to the left of the door. The figure of the Devil was also on the left immediately one entered the church. Andrew crouched down by it, touching its weird, contorted visage. "How can you explain this?" he exclaimed. "All right, the business about treasure may turn out to be so much flannel, but why should the church authorities leave this here, and that inscription? Doesn't make sense. Well, I'll push off and see if I can find the magazine lady."

After Andrew had gone I stood still for some moments, again aware of an oppressive element. The garish quality of Byzantine church decoration had never been to my taste, but Saunière's idiosyncratic touches I found disturbing. The effigies of unhappy saints with mournful eyes of black olive could be found in a hundred Catholic churches, but Saunière had decreed that all his angels should appear like lifeless dolls and there was a sinister aspect to the strange paintings he had installed. Why was Pontius Pilate shown wearing a veil and washing his hands in a white dish held by a negro? I took photographs of the Devil and of the inscription above the door, also of several paintings, but a feeling of claustrophobia became so strong that I wanted to get away from the stagnant air tinged with incense, the absurdly insipid faces and the reproachful eyes.

The graveyard seemed distinctly ordinary in comparison with Saunière's church. The sun had broken through the grey clouds and shone down on wreaths and crosses, on carefully tended graves and a stone wall over which I could see distant hills. A thrush was whistling in an almond tree and a swarm of gnats danced over a patch of nettles. At the far end of the graveyard which sloped upwards the wall was a good deal higher, and behind it there was a large house which I took to be the Villa Bethanie constructed for Saunière. There were two recently dug plots of bare earth that did not look like graves.

Halfway along the high wall I found Saunière's own gravestone, badly defaced and broken in half, lying on freshly dug earth. It looked as if several treasure-hunters had believed that the quickest route to *le trésor* was to dig up Saunière's coffin. I could read the top half of the

inscription on the stone—ICI REPOSE BERENGER SAUNIERE
CURE RENNES LE CHATEAU 1885–1917—but the words
below were undecipherable.

I photographed the stone and knelt down beside it,
touching the defaced inscription. What did I feel then?
Hard to say. Crouching there, my knees damp from the
soggy soil, as close as anyone could get to Saunière's human
remains, probably my strongest impression was of the
absolute secrets of the dead. I was reminded of an anecdote
about a pirate I had read among those on the walls of
Dave Haswell's study—how the famous Olivier le Vasseur
had flung a batch of papers at the crowd surrounding his
scaffold, crying out, "Find my treasure who can!"

I walked out of the graveyard now bathed in apricot-
coloured sunlight and past the church to look at the Villa
Bethanie. It was a good deal larger than other houses in
the village and did appear out of proportion, too big and
grand for a bachelor priest. The design was square and
plain but there was ornate stone-work round the windows
and door. A large figure of Jesus, with outstretched arms,
stood in a stone alcove level with dormer windows. The
Tour Magdala was right at the end of Saunière's garden,
perched on the corner of the hill.

The sky had cleared in the west and an orange sun was
dipping down to a range of mountains. The atmosphere
at the top of the hill was tranquil and pleasant. I could
hear the faint chugging noise of a tractor a long way off,
and a distant peal of bells, but no sound of traffic. I
wondered why the villagers living in this idyllic spot were
willing to worship in such bizzare surroundings.

21

Iron railings, with a rusty padlocked gate, surrounded the garden of the Villa Bethanie, but they ended at the Tour Magdala which had been built so that part of it overhung the hill. It was therefore possible to get close enough to the tower to give it the kind of tactile inspection which Andrew favoured. It was constructed of cream and biscuit coloured stone in medieval style, with stone mullioned windows and a battlemented parapet.

There was a stone ledge at the height of my chin. I clambered on to it and paused, wondering whether I should risk tresspassing into the grounds of the Villa Bethanie by working my way round to the right. Instead, I risked my neck by inching round the tower in the opposite direction so that I clung to it above a great drop. From that unusual vantage point I could see it was not true that exactly the same views could be obtained from the house and the tower. The Tour Magdala had been placed so that it commanded a unique prospect of the area. The panoramic view there was indeed spectacular and very beautiful, bathed in mellow light as the orange sun descended in a pale blue sky towards the mountains in the west. Clinging to the warm stone, like a reckless window-cleaner, I noticed a spot of parasitic green.

After edging my way back round the tower I spent a lot of time taking photographs of it and of the Villa Bethanie from various angles. Michelin map in hand I walked all along the edge of the hill, spotting places and also making a mental map in which I drew lines that linked them together, trying to work out what significance the unique panorama could have had for Saunière.

When Andrew appeared, walking quickly up the hill,

he moved his arms jerkily, sending a joky mock sema-
phore message. He grimaced to illustrate comic versions of
elation and despair as he came closer. "I've got good news
and bad news. Which do you want first? No, first, what
have you got?"

"I can tell you that several people haven't been intimi-
dated by all those 'Digging forbidden' signs. Old Saunière's
grave has been dug up several times I should say. And it's
quite a long time since his gravestone was first broken.
Part of the inscription has been taken off with a chisel.
And there's been some other digging in the graveyard too
—quite recently."

"That's interesting. Very interesting, as I've heard the
authoritative view that there never was any treasure. But
I'll get to that. Anything else?"

"I think there was some point in the placing of the
tower. Just there, and only there, can you see this whole
area."

"Also interesting, but this time because it coincides with
what I was told. . . ." Andrew flourished his small note-
book. "All in here, old man. I must say I've had a fascinating afternoon. Funny, because at first I thought it was
going to be a dead loss. I found Madame Brichot quite
easily, but she simply didn't want to know. Probably she's
fed-up with hearing about old Saunière. Polite enough,
asked me in, asked me to sit down, but didn't want to
help. Said she didn't have any copies of the magazine and
didn't know where I could get any."

"Which magazine? What's it called?"

"*Pegase*. Anyway, I was on the point of giving up. In
the background I could hear an old record, Django Rein-
hardt playing 'Minor Swing'—before your time I expect—
and I caught sight of this bod through the doorway, moving
about but looking as if he was listening to what I was saying. Just as I was going to get up, in he came. Monsieur
Brichot. Retired schoolmaster, scholarly type, bung-full of
local knowledge. He produced a bottle of wine and gave

me a long, detailed lecture—and I'm sure it's the real gen. Brichot is convinced that Saunière didn't find any treasure, and that the real mystery is about the identity of the people who put up the money to carry out the repairs and the building work here. 'Very rich people, people very important and well placed'—that's how he put it. And, here's the first surprise, probably people connected with Emma Calvé, the opera star."

"Ah, I wondered about that. I thought it was odd, Lumke mentioning that Saunière became friendly with Emma Calvé when he went to Paris with the coded messages. Didn't seem much point in dragging that in."

"Yes, well, one of a hundred things you and I didn't know was that both Saunière and Emma Calvé were locals. Saunière was born in Montazels, that's just where we turned off the main road. So even before he came to Rennes he lived within sight of this hill. And Emma Calvé was brought up by an aunt in Labastide-Pradines. Brichot told me that there is a strange inscription, 'ambigue formule' was how he phrased it, on her tomb in Paris. Brichot thinks that what Saunière discovered from the cyphers was not the whereabouts of treasure but certain information about a secret religious sect, the Priory or Order of Sion, a group which probably still exists today."

I took out the piece of paper which Dave Haswell had dropped on the taverna steps and read out a phrase, ". . . as a cult will survive centuries after its myths have been exposed and its sources of faith tainted. . . ."

Andrew nodded. "Yes, I remembered that. If we knew who wrote that we might have saved ourselves a trip. Those names on that list, 'The Circle', 'The Eagle's Nest', 'The Dead Man', they're just names of hills and peaks round here."

Andrew held up his notebook again and began to read : "Order of Sion linked with the Cathars. Cathars also known as the Albigencians, a name taken from the town of Albi. A powerful religious sect which flourished in the twelfth and thirteenth centuries. In their own eyes they were the only true Christians and nearer than Roman Catholics to the traditions of the early Christians. Their theology was based on a dualistic belief in an evil principle in the Universe which limited God's power. That two opposed powers or principles are active in the Universe. The evil being was sometimes known as the Monster of Chaos, which partook of the nature of man, fish, bird or beast. But at the same time it was a spirit which had no beginning or end. Satan had created the material world and the flesh, and man's task was to liberate his spirit, the good part of him, from his material envelope. The Cathar teaching about Christ was that he had appeared in this world merely as a phantom—his mission was to teach the doctrine of salvation and to warn mankind that the God of the Old Testament was really a demon who had created the material world. Christ's true mission, however, had been elsewhere, in superior worlds, and his crucifixion in this world was fictitious. Important belief was that the Devil ruled the material world, so he was called 'Rex Mundi'."

"Did Brichot mean that the Priory of Sion is the present-day equivalent of the Albigencians?"

Andrew pulled a doubtful expression and thought for a moment. "He was a bit vague about that. But according to him this whole area was a stronghold of the Albigencians at one time. He said there are a lot of churches round here, at Couiza, Arques, Bezu, that have signs linking them with the Albigencians. Even at Montazels, where Saunière was born, there are some 'mysterious stone figures'."

"So, no treasure?"

"According to Brichot, no chance. I mean, here's a man who's lived in this village for sixty years with a scholarly interest in such things. He must have seen dozens of hopeful treasure-hunters poking round here but he's convinced there's nothing to it, made the point that

Saunière did regular trips to Paris and these coincided with cash being spent. He even came up with one possible name, said that a wealthy friend of Emma Calvé, a Stanislas de Guaita, may have put up some of the money."

"Well, I must say the idea of a secret cult paying to have an old Cathar church re-built makes more sense than buried treasure. That would explain why the angels are made to look like lifeless dolls and the Devil dominates the entrance. . . . Madame Brichot said nothing, not even when her husband had told you of this?"

"Not a word. Just sat there looking alert and watchful, although I suppose she must have heard that stuff dozens of times. Occasionally her eyes flashed as if she could add something if she had wanted to—she's got very eloquent, very dark brown eyes, the colour of Marmite. When Brichot mentioned the name de Guaita she suddenly looked apprehensive. Oh yes, there was something else, something I didn't write down. Apparently there was quite a bit of publicity in the newspapers about this whole affair."

"If it got into the French nationals it may have rated an inch in the English papers. Perhaps that's how Haswell and Reardon got on to it. I thought it was unlikely that they would have read some obscure French magazine."

"What we've got to face is the probability that Haswell and Reardon came here hoping to find Solomon's gold and they realised it was all balls. Ten to one when they were in Corfu they were off on another track, something quite different. In which case we've wasted our time and cash."

"I shan't burst into tears over that. I wouldn't have missed this trip. Okay, Brichot may be right about the treasure angle, but we are close to a real mystery here."

"Yes, I know what you mean. It's an attractive village but the atmosphere is eerie."

Sunset had produced a deepening pink and rose sky which was dyeing everything about us a paler pink as we made our way down the hill. We stopped for some moments outside the rusty garden gate of the Villa Bethanie. Apart from the stone figure of Christ, the house was similar to thousands of French provincial villas of the same period, but, framed by a rose-coloured sky, it seemed to me to have an enigmatic look. Not normally given to suggestible imaginings, staring at the blank windows I had the strong sensation that the house regarded us with satisfaction. Two more intruders were about to leave the village without having got to the bottom of Saunière's mysteries.

As we turned the bend in the path by the church I saw a silver-coloured BMW with a Swedish registration plate parked at a spot much higher than the one I had chosen. It moved off silently as we approached. Parked so close to the church, it was obvious that it had brought other visitors anxious to view the results of the priest's bizarre activities; I wondered how many tourists came to puzzle over the inscription, the effigy of the Devil, the lifeless angels and defaced tombs, then departed not much the wiser.

22

CARCASSONNE. Monday, 4th October 1976.

A *Pizzeria* right at the top of the old part of the city was Andrew's choice for our evening meal after the expedition to Rennes. Walking there we crossed over a drawbridge and went through a gateway in the ancient, massive stone walls. I was hungry and had had enough sight-seeing for one day. After leaving Rennes Andrew had insisted on our making a quick trip to Montazels, which had been a waste of time as the only stone carvings we had found were Tritons on the village fountain. But Andrew's appetite for such activities seemed insatiable; armed with a brochure about Carcassonne he had picked up in the Hotel du Pont Vieux, he appeared to want to give me a guided tour.

"Look," he said, waving the pamphlet, "they mention Carcassonne and 'le drame Cathare de 1209'. So the Cathars were here too."

"Can't really see it in this light. I'll look later."

Although I had enjoyed Andrew's company during the day, I knew that if I had a magician's wand I would have changed him into Jane Mackmurdo as all I wanted now was a quiet meal and bed. Fair enough, I thought, because I'm sure he would do the same with me.

Walking up the narrow street lined with small shops, he continued to read part of the brochure out loud : "*Au centre de cet écrin de pierre, un joyau, la Basilique Saint-Nazaire. . . .*" But the recital tailed off as he became distracted by the shops, most of which were still open though the customers were few and the shopkeepers looked tired and apathetic. He kept pointing at the windows. Nearly all the shops appeared to be tourist traps selling identical rubbish. He insisted on stopping outside one that was stocked with gaudy religious mementos. The painfully slow walk reminded me of making similarly halting progess along the path to Axel Munthe's villa in Anacapri, being pestered to buy amateurish water-colours and gimcrack musical boxes that churned out "The Isle of Capri".

When we were finally seated in the *Pizzeria*, Andrew looked at me closely over the menu and asked, "Tired?"

"Hungry." It had been eight hours since our picnic lunch and though I would not have wanted to mention it I had missed not having an afternoon cup of tea. Yes, I thought, middle age has set in. Adventures are fine for some; others are better suited to a life of routine with regular cups of tea and coffee. As I studied the menu I thought about Jane Mackmurdo. Undoubtedly she had been disillusioned with me during the one night we had spent together. In Corfu I had probably given a rather false impression : the romantic who liked to listen to Strauss in the moonlight; the muscular ex-boxer who looked his best in a swimming costume; the light-hearted bloke who got drunk and dived off a cliff. In Spanish Place she had seen me as I was for fifty weeks in a year, a very ordinary chap caught up in the syndrome of middle age, becoming set in his ways. As I brooded on the dim chance of ever seeing Jane again, I felt an expression of weariness and depression setting on my face like a sour grimace, and rubbed it with both hands.

Andrew shrugged. "What do you think? Do you want a starter? Or just a pizza and lots of Beaujolais?"

"That's fine, but let's ask for the wine right away."

The young woman had already brought us a long loaf and a plate of olives. Within a minute she returned with a litre of new Beaujolais.

I drank some of the wine and looked round the *Pizzeria*. The premises of an old bakery had been changed into a restaurant with the minimum of fuss, using plenty of white-wash and white paint and making a feature of the large oven which dominated the centre of the dining-room.

A girlish-looking boy with shoulder-length hair was playing a guitar in the far corner. Most of the customers appeared to be in their twenties. I thought they would have been surprised to hear that the rather dull-looking middle-aged Englishmen had spent their afternoon touching a Devil, inspecting graves, climbing a tower and investigating a secret religious cult.

Andrew filled my glass again and said, "You know, Rennes may end up as a tourist place. Could happen. Charas and Yanks. Japs with lots of cameras. Fact is, I'm surprised it hasn't already caught on. Lots of potential really. A shop by the church selling effigies of the Devil and copies of the parchments. Monsieur Brichot would make a splendid guide."

"What struck me about the place, what I keep thinking about, is the fact that Saunière died in 1917. I mean, I wonder what happened between then and now? In the twenties and thirties—did anybody get interested in the affair then? People must sometimes have come to the village by chance, casually strolled into the church. What could they have made of it?"

"What I've been thinking about is the gaps in Brichot's version. For all we know he may serve a purpose—he produces a reasonable-sounding story to fob off people who insist on poking their noses in. Just enough of a tale to satisfy."

Andrew produced his notebook and studied it for a while. He looked slightly puzzled and said, "That's odd. Something I specially meant to tell you and must have forgotten. Brichot did say that in the Bibliothèque Nationale in Paris there's a book which lists all the descendants of King Dagobert III, and also gives the names of members of the Priory of Sion, including Nicolas Flamel, Isaac Newton and Victor Hugo. Also Debussy, who was a friend of Emma Calvé. I suppose we could check up on that. Do you know anyone there?"

"We've sold them some books, had some correspondence

with their 'Service des Acquisitions'. I can easily write to them."

The litre bottle had been emptied as if by magic and a replacement was brought at the same time as the pizzas, which looked succulent and overbrimmed large plates.

For a while we ate and drank in silence. The Beaujolais was particularly good, the kind of wine that is rushed to London at great expense to please the rich customers of over-priced restaurants. That knowledge added zest to drinking it at a very modest cost in Carcassonne. With the faintest hint of slurring Andrew said, "Don't know about you, old man, but I've enjoyed this trip. . . . All this stuff about the Cathars. . . . Two hundred of them were burnt at Montsegur in 1244 you know. . . . Siege of their mountain stronghold. . . . Others crept down. . . . Escaped. . . ."

Andrew had already bombarded me with similar information when I had been driving back from Rennes-le-Château, and I was beginning to feel as if facts about the Middle Ages were coming out of my ears. I kept nodding at regular intervals but made no other contribution to the conversation; I found that a considerable effort was necessary just to look interested—like Mrs Findlay-Duncan after drinks in Nissaki. Tiredness and a litre of Beaujolais had combined to have a drugging effect.

When our meal was over a crowd of youngsters called out *"Bon nuit"* and Andrew waved a long loaf at them; I went out of the door in a daze, grateful that we had not driven to the old city. Andrew banged into the doorway and said something, partly incoherent, about the "Monster of Chaos". He sniffed the night air. "We haven't made much snakes and ladders progress I'm afraid, old man. Madame Brichot was worried. Perhaps that's significant? Savvy?"

"Perhaps." The bed in my room at the Hotel du Pont Vieux seemed infinitely desirable. My legs felt wooden, and walking down the steeply sloping street became a matter of stumping along like a man with artificial legs.

The shops were all shut but some of the windows were still lit, and once more Andrew had trouble in resisting their allure. He kept stopping and making comments that I did not take in at all. He made very slow weaving progress, and by the time I reached the drawbridge he was so far behind that I could no longer hear his footsteps. I stopped for a minute, looking down into the dry bed of the moat. Even in a semi-stupor the fortified entrance to the ancient city seemed a romantic spot under a sky full of stars. I tried to imagine how it must have been to look out from where I was standing and see the armies of Simon de Montfort slowly wending their way across the plain below to start their siege campaign.

A muffled cry for help dispelled these fanciful imaginings and cleared my head. A second cry injected enough adrenalin to sober me up completely. My heart pumped quickly and my fists clenched. I ran back over the drawbridge and through the dark gateway. At the entrance of an alley I saw Andrew wrestling with a very tall man. The big man with blond hair towered over Andrew and had one hand round his throat. Andrew's face looked mortally pale and blood trickled from his nose.

I punched the tall man low down in his side. When he turned round he was six inches shorter and groggy with pain. I tapped his head back with two left jabs in quick succession. He lunged at me with a chopping right hand that caught my ear and shoulder, but I hit him with a left hook that rocked his head back. He was strong but pain was preventing him from thinking straight. Coming forward again he shook his head as if in a daze, and I knew I had him, a presentiment that rarely fails experienced boxers. He was trying to get close enough to grapple with me but I stepped round so that I was retreating uphill and found it easy to dodge his long arms. I caught him with so many left hooks it was like punching a bag.

When the big man threw a wild right at me he stumbled and I caught him with a flurry of blows, a left to the side of his head, a right to the jaw and a punishing left to his throat. He stumbled a second time and I knew exactly how numb and useless his legs felt. As he moved forward he was out of control and I leant into him and connected with a right cross that must have changed the angle of his nose. It was the kind of punch that sends back a message of its success along the arm before the victim hits the ground.

As the blond man went down sideways into the gutter I ran down to where Andrew was standing, propped up against the side of a house, holding his neck with both hands.

"Run! Start running!" I shouted. Andrew looked as if he might want to debate the point but I pushed him in the direction of the gateway and ran behind him with a guiding hand on his shoulder. The steepness of the slope beyond the drawbridge gave us a momentum that sent us racing down towards the deserted car park. We pounded along the road that led eventually to our hotel, but after a hundred yards I pushed Andrew round a corner to the left and then turned right again so that we were in a quiet street running parallel with the road.

"All right, we can stop now."

"I'm winded."

"I know. It's okay now. No one coming."

"Good God! Did you really think he was going to get up after that and chase us?"

"No, but I didn't fancy the idea of spending a night in the cells arguing the toss with a bunch of gendarmes."

Andrew nodded and stood silent for some moments, getting his breath back. Blood had stopped trickling from his nose but there were lumps round his eyes, and I knew from experience that he would look a good deal worse in the morning.

Suddenly he grinned, though I could see it was a painful process, and said, "You caught him with the old one-two all right. It was goodnight nurse then."

"No, I was lucky—started off with a low punch. Twenty years ago I could have tamed him. Now I'd need a whip and a chair."

"You've got a good left hook."

"Well, perhaps just a chair."

"Now do you believe in my story about the blond giant at Nissaki?"

"That was the same man?"

"I don't make a habit of encounters with blond giants—of course it was the same man. He stepped out of the alley and I could tell I was for it. Bloody maniac. Grabbed me by the throat and said, 'Do you know who it is?' Kept repeating that one sentence over and over—like a madman. I didn't know what he was talking about and I couldn't get anything out anyway. He's definitely a Swedish madman."

"Why Swedish?"

"I can jabber it a bit, *Hur mycket är klockan?*—What is the time? That kind of thing. After he'd asked me the question 'Do you know who it is?' about six times he tried it in Swedish, *'Vet ni vem det är?'* He's Swedish, I'm sure. And a psycho. The pee is silent as in bathing."

I grinned. I had to admire someone who could take a beating and end up making a joke. Then I remembered something I had seen at Rennes.

"There was a silver-coloured BMW with a Swedish plate at Rennes—it slid off just as we came down the hill from the church."

"Yes, I have a nasty feeling, old man, that we've actually encountered one of 'the demented friends of the late Mr Townshend'. And that there is method in their madness."

"Funny—this morning we thought we were on a treasure trail. Now Monsieur Brichot, with a wave of a wand, seems to have made the treasure vanish, but Townshend's demented friends turn out to be real after all."

"We can't be positive yet about the treasure. Haswell

and Reardon were in Corfu looking for something. . . . It's my fault—we went off at half-cock coming here before I'd seen Peter Lumke."

"I don't regret the trip. Not one hundred per cent pleasurable perhaps, and you're going to have a black eye in the morning, but it hasn't been a waste of time."

"I'll keep after Lumke when we get back."

"And what do we do about the Swedish psycho?"

"Good question. I can't see myself going into the police-station at Cookham to lodge a complaint about a blond giant who gave me a nasty look in Nissaki and tried to choke me in Carcassonne. What do you suggest?"

"Nothing tonight. My head's beginning to ache and I can't think straight. I need a shower and bed. You need to get a cold wet cloth on your face and keep it there for a bit."

23

"Vet ni vem det är?" "Do you know who it is?" This question haunted me for three days after returning from France. I pushed it around in my mind but could not see how it fitted in with either the mystery of Rennes-le-Château or the tragedy at Nissaki. The encounter with the Swedish giant had proved that there was some link between the two places, but my mind could not take the leap between them. I found myself saying *"Vet ni vem det är?"* as I shaved and as I went to bed.

Our flight back from France was uneventful, though Andrew's battered face caused some eyebrows to be raised. Indeed, the flight-control officer at Cherbourg had seemed more interested in Andrew's black eye than in our flight plan to cross the Channel.

When I got back to Lilliput House I found there had been a satisfactory haul of business letters, but nothing of personal interest. An official order, stamped "Urgent" and "Rush", had arrived from the Canadian University Library for Dolek's Russian pamphlets. It looked as if they knew they were on to a bargain, and wanted to clinch the deal before we had second thoughts. And my indefatigable assistant had also sold to an American collector one hundred books concerning Dr Johnson and his circle.

I've always found packing books an enjoyable task, and solving the logistical problems regarding the Johnson collection, where the books ranged in size from the folio Dictionary to some duodecimos, kept me busy for two hours and took my mind off the nagging question "Do you know who it is?" Sending off the Dolek collection was a different matter; it was easily packed into two wine-cartons and involved hardly any physical labour, but I tackled it with melancholy thoughts about the futility of man's achievements.

It was predictable, psychologically, that when I returned from the Post Office I immediately phoned Jane Mackmurdo. There were introductory clicks but no reply. I hung on for a few minutes, listening to the sound of the bell, imagining it ringing and echoing in the large, rather sombre Spanish Place flat, hoping that she might be washing her hair and would finally emerge from the bathroom to cheer me up with an enthusiastic response to my call.

I had used the upstairs telephone, and when I went down to the shop Mary asked, "Did you have trouble with that call? There's definitely something wrong with the phone. All those clicks. Very irritating."

I made just a nodding assent to the complaint about the telephone; my mind was taken up with more important matters than phones that were not functioning properly. I had remembered an old and incomplete encyclopaedia down in the basement. It lacked only one volume out of ten so I thought I would be very unlucky if I could not find any information in it regarding the Albigencians/Cathars.

There was an entry under

CATHARI

a widespread heresy extending among the Gnostics of the Middle Ages, gave rise to this name which signified 'pure' and came from the Greek. The Cathari assumed different names in different countries. In the east they were called Bogomils or Paulicians; in the west they were called Paterini, because they held their meetings where the rag-pickers used to meet, in the Street Pateria. The heresy first started in the tenth and lasted till the middle of the fourteenth century, when it was rooted out by the Inquisition. The Cathari were divided into two classes, the 'Perfecti' and the 'Credentes'. The Perfecti were saints on earth to whom the Believers gave unquestioning obedience. They believed that Satan was the ruler of this world, which was a kind of Purgatory or Hell, but they believed in the ultimate salvation of mankind. . . .

Andrew had said he was going to contact Peter Lumke as soon as possible, so I copied out this further information about the Cathars to post to him. The "Monster of Chaos" and "Rex Mundi" had the ring of nonsense in my ears, but how could one dismiss ideas that apparently had appealed to the great Isaac Newton?

One evening that week after seeing Erich von Stroheim's film *Greed*, which had eluded me for years, I felt in a restless mood, unwilling to listen to music or read. I wrote out all the fragments of conversation I had overheard in Nissaki on a foolscap sheet of paper, then added other information that had come my way since returning from Corfu. I made a great effort to keep it neat, using a stilted attempt at calligraphic script, and in the end it was quite legible, a large page crammed with fragments of conversation such as Barbara Haswell's report of a break-in at her flat where "At first it looked as if they hadn't taken anything" and Dainty Haswell's final comment on his brother: "I never seed him so serious. Mind, he really needed the loot . . . he'd put this uvver young tart, this Eileen, in the pudden club."

Adding afterthoughts, reducing the size of my writing to get in even later thoughts in the margin, I finished up with what looked like a manuscript draft page from the pen of a painstaking novelist. I stared at it for a long time without arriving at any solution. The irritating idea that the answer lay in my subconscious nagged me; a place and a voice were shadowy factors, the significance of which I could not dredge up. When I finally went to bed, my last thought took the shape of a question: "Do you know who it is?"

24

Lᴵᴸᴸᴵᴘᴜᴛ Hᴏᴜꜱᴇ. 9th October 1976.

Early in the morning, before the commuters and shoppers arrive, London has the busily absorbed atmosphere of a village. It is a time I particularly enjoy and on this eventful Saturday which began in an ordinary way I went out for a stroll. I wanted to buy some croissants; other local inhabitants were on similar chores, and I chatted with two neighbours, and watched fish being unloaded at the shop at the top of Duke of York Street and massive cheeses being rolled off a lorry in Jermyn Street.

When I returned to Lilliput House I took my time over croissants and coffee. Mary Carpenter had gone off for a long weekend at Rye and I did not expect our little backwater to be invaded by many bibliophiles anxious to purchase our wares. In my experience book-collectors are a not very energetic race and prefer to have their attention drawn to possible bargains before walking round to Mason's Yard.

While lingering over a second cup of coffee I looked at an old coloured post-card which had taken my fancy when it had dropped out of a scrap-book. It showed a street scene outside the Restaurant Vielle in Paris, circa 1930. A priest in black robe and cloak chatted to a road-sweeper in a Reckitts-blue tunic. A small boy wearing a brown suit, gaiters and beret held a Pomeranian on a long lead. Two fashionable ladies, conscious of the camera, posed elegantly. A vanished world, quite different from the Paris I knew. I picked up a pen and wrote Jane Mackmurdo's Spanish Place address on the blank side of the card in the crabbed italic hand that I had imposed on a natural tendency to scrawl.

Dear Jane. Why are you there while I am here? One of those Puzzles that Life likes to pose, being endlessly inventive when it comes to arranging that no one is really happy for long. Should be wise to meet again? Another Conundrum.

The telephone rang and put an end to my pointless scribbling. I said Hello. There were the now customary, irritating clicks and for a moment the line seemed to go dead as if the caller had been disconnected. Then a momentarily blurred voice.

"Hello—hello Harry! My, you're an elusive fellow! This is the third time I've called recently...."

Over the phone Alec Harvey's voice exuded confidence and energy. He stimulated a flow of chumpish epigrams in me and I felt like asking if he'd found wood-worm in the Shakespeare bust he'd claimed from me at a discount. Instead I mildly explained that I'd been out a lot and my assistant had gone off on a short holiday.

"Well, Harry, there's something that should be said I think, but preferably not over the phone. I'm in Lincoln's Inn Fields talking shop at the moment, and later on I'm off to Perthshire, but I can pop out for five minutes. Can you meet me in the gardens here? On the north side, by the Margaret Macdonald seat? Something that will interest you, I'm sure. You can park in New Square quite easily on a Saturday...."

I told Harvey I would be in Lincoln's Inn within twenty minutes. I put my breakfast things in the sink, cleaned my teeth, and popped the card marked "Closed" on the shop door. Ten to one some country customer who only visited us annually would choose this Saturday morning to make his pilgrimage and heap insults on our small premises. As I was leaving I noticed a note to me in Mary Carpenter's neat hand which had fallen on to the floor.

Harry—Just to say there is definitely something wrong

with our phone. I called the operator and the Engineer's Department. They are sending someone on Monday to see about it. They could not make a more definite time than "in the morning", but I shall be back by then. . . .

The traffic going towards the City was light and I reached New Square within ten minutes of leaving Mason's Yard. I parked my dusty Lancia next to a gleaming apple-green Rolls, and thought for the tenth time that I must get the dented wing repaired. Undoubtedly Alec Harvey would be able to recommend a former client with a shady background, expert at disguising cars.

The sky above Lincoln's Inn was a wishy-washy blue, like that in a faded water-colour. As I sat waiting on the Margaret Macdonald seat, beneath a carved stone representation of a woman with outstretched arms protecting children, I watched clouds infiltrating the sky. Some flimsy wisps of cloud blew over without stopping; others built up into pillow-like shapes, then into improbable castles and finally made uninteresting maps of snow-covered land.

I heard footsteps on the path and looked round to see a blind man slowly making his way towards me, tapping with his white stick. A moment later, with brisker steps on the asphalt, Alec Harvey appeared from the same gate, wearing a thin brown tweed suit with a waistcoat and a brown felt hat. I pondered why I would feel slightly "dressed up" in that outfit while he appeared relaxed and perfectly dressed for his trip to Scotland.

" 'Morning, Harry. Not a particularly good one. Looks as if the summer has finally given up. Lamentable timing I must say."

"Perhaps it's quite different in Perthshire."

"I don't think it is, actually." Harvey sat down, extended his long legs and extracted a slip of paper from an inside pocket.

"Old friend of mine, Freddy Williams—a former County Court Judge in Northants—has died. Left a cellar of excellent wine, some nice books, and a youngish widow with expensive tastes. I want one of his books—Gascoigne's *A Hundred Sundrie Flowres*. No doubt I could buy it directly from Mrs Williams, but I don't think that would be fair. I should like you to act for me—fix the market price."

"Of course. Just let me know which day."

There was nothing about going to Northampton to buy a rare book which could not be mentioned on the phone, so I was convinced that Harvey had something else up his elegant sleeve.

"Good, good. I'll set that in train."

Alec Harvey nodded judicially and made a minute notation on the slip of paper, replaced it in his pocket and extracted what appeared to be another piece of paper. He glanced at it for a moment, as if it had some fascination for him, before handing it to me.

"Do you recognise her?"

I looked at a photograph of a young woman on a stone seat. She wore a long dress of dark velvet with white lace collar and cuffs. A twisted band of some other material served as a belt. The dress was old-fashioned but I could not possibly have placed the period. The woman was very attractive, with mid-brown hair that looked lighter on the top because it was lit by a shaft of sunlight. Her hair was done in an unusual style, appearing as if it might be piled up from behind. She had a wide forehead, large dark eyes and a sensitive mouth. She had a book on her lap but was looking directly at the camera. She was smiling slightly but her expression was a subtle one, impossible to describe adequately, combining faint amusement, calmness and some other quality—perhaps confidence or assurance. It was a memorable face and I knew I had not seen her.

"No. Should I?"

"Well, I don't know I'm sure. But what we have here is a rare snapshot of someone with a strong prejudice against being photographed. A good likeness still, I'm credibly informed, though it was taken over thirty years ago. . . ."

Alec Harvey paused as if for dramatic effect. I could easily visualise him doing the same thing in court, judging his timing with the jury, looking round to make sure he had their full attention. He had the reputation of having held his own with Lord Chief Justice Goddard, and I believed the story. He took the photograph from me and held it up by one corner.

"Viola Ismay Ormond Townshend. Really, Harry, you are playing this game with your cards so close to your chest I don't quite know where we are. Next thing you'll tell me is that, despite your 'idle curiosity' about the family, you do not know that Miss Townshend now lives in Corfu from where you have only just returned. She owns a very handsome villa there, I'm told. At a place called Aghios Stephanos."

As he drawled out the place name my mind instantly filled with images. White rocks and cliffs festooned with mesembryanthemum. Dazzling white stone walls in fierce sunlight. Then a darker image of two corpses huddled on the floor of a fishing-boat. And a coil of rope and a rope ladder in a smaller boat. Suddenly I knew the answer to the mystery of the treasure. It did not lie submerged in a wreck off Kouloura or Karagol Point—Theo and Evstratios had been right in contemptuously dismissing such an idea. The treasure, in the minds of the two Cockney adventurers, had been hidden in the villa at Aghios Stephanos. Their underwater equipment had been a blind. Their ropes and rope ladder had been for scaling the cliffs and walls. Somewhere on the trail of the supposed treasure of Rennes-le-Château they had come on strong evidence of a link with the Townshend family and, desperate for cash (I remembered Dainty Haswell saying of his brother "I never seed him so serious. Mind, he really needed the loot . . ."), they had become determined to have it. Now I felt sure that the Swedish giant's repeated question "Do you know who

145

it is?" had been framed to see if we knew of the link with Viola Townshend.

"I've seen her house."

"Ah, I thought you might."

"Only through a locked gate, peering in like a Bisto Kid."

"Yes, I was informed that visitors were definitely not encouraged. You see your curiosity stimulated my own. . . ."

He paused, and again there was something theatrical in his drawling voice. He could have been outlining charges made against one of his clients, to demonstrate their palpable absurdity. He did not know that, while I absorbed this impression, an image of two corpses kept reforming in my mind.

"Therefore I made inquiries. And I happened to find someone who once was a friend of the family. No names, no pack drill, but he did know them quite well for a time. Indeed, he was a guest at their house in Dorset. Hence the photograph which was taken there. He told me that the brother and sister—always a slightly odd pair apparently—were *very* close. More like husband and wife he said. A church on their estate was burnt down mysteriously in their father's time. After that their cottages were left to become derelict. Now even their ancestral home is much dilapidated. Victor died in Geneva this summer, from a heart attack, as you know. Apparently Viola leads the life of a recluse in Corfu."

Alec Harvey put Viola's photograph on the seat between us. As I looked down on her face I remembered a dictionary entry about the Cathari: "The name signifies 'pure' and comes from the Greek 'a cleansing purification'." I could well believe that some of the late Mr Townshend's demented friends had been over-zealous in protecting the secrets of the Cathar cult, but I found it hard to credit that this woman had taken any part in criminal activities. Harvey's few sentences on the subject had acted like the crucial adjustment of a lens in a microscope, making clear what

146

had previously been blurred. I now felt sure that the Townshend family, probably for many generations, had acted as paymasters supporting the Albigencians. I was certain too that the treasure Dave Haswell imagined to be kept at Aghios Stephanos did not exist in a portable form. The Townshend fortune, consisting of land in England and funds in Swiss banks, would not be available to desperate adventurers. Reluctantly I faced the fact that I should now have to go to the police with my miscellaneous odds and ends of information. It seemed probable that Townshend's friends had been forewarned of the activities of Haswell and Reardon; and it was quite likely that the unlucky pair had been killed in making their attempt to rob the villa. For a moment I considered blurting out all I knew to Alec Harvey—obviously he would be able to give me sage advice. Then I decided to talk to Andrew Foster before taking any irrevocable steps.

Harvey had undone his jacket and was fishing about in various inside pockets, as if demonstrating the superb quality of its lining and the great care given to its cut. He extracted a card from a ticket pocket and took out a slim gold pen.

"I thought you might care to see the location of the Townshend house in Dorset. Unusual in that it is so difficult to approach."

Harvey's writing was as minute as that of Andrew Foster, and just as precise and legible. As he drew tiny lines a Lilliputian map began to take shape on the card. He inserted three dots in an ascending line and then hesitated before adding a fourth.

"Toller Fratrum, Toller Porcorum, Toller Whelme— they more or less follow the road from Dorchester to Crewkerne. Toller Parva is placed there, midway between the roads to Yeovil and Sherborne. Can be approached from either direction but only on foot. I'm told the Townshends' road from the A37 was closed years ago, possibly contravening some ancient right of way. There's been trouble over that. . . ."

Harvey brooded over the card, pedantically correcting a twist in the road towards Sherborne. When he looked up he gave me one of his rare grins, as he had at his party when he'd seen me flirting with the blonde actress.

"In law, I'm told, there *is* a right of way to the site of the church, though this is still being disputed. . . . You know what lawyers are. But I suppose someone who wanted to badly enough could tramp along it."

Harvey gave me the tiny map and pocketed the photograph. Then he took out a gold repeater watch and regarded its old-fashioned face solemnly. "Good God, Harry! Have we really been here twenty minutes? E'en now I should be speeding towards Heathrow. Goodbye. I hope I've been helpful."

25

There was no mob of frustrated book-collectors demonstrating in front of my tiny premises when I returned to Mason's Yard but, as I parked outside the shop, I could hear the telephone ringing. I imagined that one of our customers had found the "Closed" notice irritating and had gone round the corner to a phone-box to express his annoyance.

My mind was still busy with all the new ramifications of the Townshend affair. I had a penchant for reveries but I did not like having my mind so absorbed that I was unaware of driving from Holborn to Piccadilly. I realised that Alec Harvey had demonstrated extraordinary tact in taking so much trouble to give me information without inquiring what my interest was. He had urbane qualities that I envied; I now regretted not having taken him into my confidence. Undoubtedly he could have shown me the path to take.

I got out of the car practically in slow motion, feeling as I had done years before when I'd taken too many punches. An appropriate boxing joke came into my mind: "It's all right, I can take Rocky in the next round." "Listen, you *are* Rocky."

As I picked up the phone I was confident that I would hear a reproachful voice. Instead there was a click and then annoying silence. I said my number, then my name. Silence. I hung on, mentally cursing the telephone service, repeating "Hello, Harry Gilmour here."

Another click, and I heard "Hello Harry" in a feminine voice that I recognised with a tiny stab of excitement. It was just the sort of treatment to wake me from that punch-drunk feeling.

My "Hello Jane" came out in a surprisingly non-committal tone, probably due to nerves.

"Oh, I'm glad I hung on. Anyway I was going to try again in fifteen minutes. I wanted to explain. About the other evening. I'm sorry about that."

"I thought it was my fault. Something I'd done or something I hadn't done. Or just me."

"Of course not, you fool. It was me. There had been—someone else. Anyway, that's all over now. I'm fine and I want—I hope to see you. I went to Yorkshire for a few days, sorted myself out during long walks on the moors. . . ."

She paused but I could tell she was going to add something else so I waited. When she spoke again her tone had changed slightly, was less serious.

"So-o—if you're inclined—we'll start a new chapter. Perhaps a short book."

"Of course I want to see you."

Yes, I'm selfish, I thought. Dorothy's verdict is fair enough. I'm feckless and selfish and I want to see Jane again regardless of the consequences. Undoubtedly it will only be a chapter, but then nothing lasts long.

"Great. . . . I had a second reason for hanging on to the phone. Andrew Foster rang me, said he'd been trying to contact you and asked if I'd try. He was at an airfield in wildest Suffolk or somewhere. He said it was blowing a gale there. Anyway, the message he wanted me to pass on was that he was going to fly to Dorset this afternoon. He wanted you to meet him there, at a place called Toller Parva. Does that make sense?"

"Yes, I know the place. I'll drive there."

"Well, I shan't be going out, so I'll man the phone here in case either of you wants to ring again. Andrew said he thought you'd find the answer to the puzzle in Dorset. Sounds very mysterious."

"It is a bit—and very complicated. But I'll tell you when I see you next."

"Shall you be able to get back to London this evening?"

"Yes. London to Dorchester takes me about three hours."

"Well don't drive too fast. Come back safe and call in at Spanish Place. Won't matter if it's late. I shall cook a beef casserole. It's my only good dish—and it will keep for hours—like me. Goodbye darling."

She had rung off before I could reply.

26

THE DRIVE FROM London to Dorset was even quicker than I had expected. I knew the first part of the journey like the back of my hand, for the road led towards Stonehenge and our cottage near Wardour Castle, until it diverged for Andover and Salisbury. On the straight Roman road to Salisbury I sped along; it was lunch-time, there was very little traffic and the temptation to exceed the speed limit was irresistible.

I stopped for five minutes in the beautiful Cranborne Chase area, near Sixpenny Handley, and ate a piece of cheese, a croissant and a Cox's Orange Pippin as I compared an ordnance survey map with Alec Harvey's attempt at cartography. His drawing was remarkably good. He had hesitated over the placing of Toller Parva but he could not have done it more accurately with the ordnance map in front of him. It appeared to me that my best bet was to take the Sherborne road from Dorchester to a hamlet named Forston, from which a lane led towards Toller Parva, though it petered out before reaching it.

One disturbing incident marred the last stage of the journey. As I drove through Puddletown I listened to the news on the radio, and it included a brief report that a small private aircraft had crashed in a field near Elstree and the pilot had been killed. I knew there were hundreds of light aircraft in Britain but for a while I had the unpleasant nagging impression that it might be Andrew's Cessna which had crashed and burst into flames.

The sky was uniformly grey, and when I had got out of the car to stretch my legs and eat my snack I had noticed how strong the wind blowing from the north-east had become. Early falling leaves were dancing in the air as I followed the course of the River Cerne out of Dorchester, and the wind made a blustery noise against the car windows.

I parked just off the road in Forston. Map in hand, I soon found the ancient lane that led due west up a hill. The grassy track, hedged with blackberry bushes, turned into a chalk path strewn with flints, and then again into rougher grass between hawthorn and furze bushes and harebells and tottergrass. It was indeed an unusual part of the country, appearing remote and deserted although within two miles of a busy road. I saw a ramshackle old barn and there were signs that a tractor occasionally used the path I was taking, but there were no cottages or farm-houses to be seen; the only sounds were of larks singing high above and the wind that sighed and moaned.

At the top of the hill a copse grew along a ridge. The track turned in a southerly direction to skirt the trees and become more overgrown with stunted bushes and rank grass.

Picking my way between mole hills and brambles I began to wonder if I had got lost, then the trees thinned out and I saw a steep slope leading down to the hamlet of Toller Parva. The blackened ruins of the church were partly covered with ivy. A holly-tree grew out of the ruins and I could imagine it in June with white blossom full of bees, looking like a minor miracle, life springing up from destruction. Three derelict cottages, without doors and windows, stood close by the bare foundations of other cottage walls. The big house, a fine stone building with a terrace, showed no sign of dilapidation at a distance.

Old Court faced south. On its east side, beyond the ruined church, there was an area of parkland where I imagined Andrew might be able to land his Cessna. Our meeting was likely to be a rather dismal affair, with my strong suspicion of how Haswell and Reardon had died, together with my conviction that the treasure had vanished like fairy gold. It now seemed inevitable that we would become involved in police inquiries. Nevertheless I was still keen to find out whether seeing the Townshend house would provide us with any answers.

A few sunflowers sprouted between massive clumps of nettles and waist-high grass in the cottage garden plots. There were some wizened apple-trees in shrouds of ivy and lichen. The wind seemed to howl with particular intensity about the broken roofs and walls. In the east an ominous wedge of dark grey sky had appeared. I thought that Andrew would need all his skill in landing at Toller Parva.

The turf near to the house was springy and cropped. As I got nearer to Old Court I could see signs of neglect; there were gaps in the attractive Victorian iron screen which ran along the stone wall, and two of the windows on the south side of the house were boarded up while others appeared to be screened inside with green cloth. The iron gates, which stood between lofty stone piers surmounted by huge stone balls, were broken and propped open by metal stays.

I walked through the gates, and what had once been a rose garden, with a melancholy sensation. Within thirty feet the neglected house had an unhealthy look about it, like a patient who was being refused treatment. I could not understand why Viola Townshend should prefer to see the house disintegrate rather than let other people live there.

A fluted stone hood over the stout oak door had a Crusader's shield carved at its centre; it looked as if an inscription or motto on the shield had been obliterated.

I walked slowly round the house, coming across a stone bench on the terrace, perhaps the one on which Viola Townshend had been photographed some thirty years ago. Immediately afterwards I saw evidence to link her family with the Cathars : on the west wall of the house there was a finely carved stone replica of the Poussin painting.

A french window was propped open, like a trap for the unwary, and the temptation to enter was too strong for me to resist. I stepped inside to find a large, lofty room from which several paintings had been removed, leaving faded shapes on the Chinese wallpaper, though it was still scantily furnished; even more surprising to me were the signs that the room had been the scene of a recent meeting. Dust-covers had been thrown on the bare wooden floor, and chairs stood askew with flattened cushions. There were empty glasses on a small table. A great pile of wood-ash filled the hearth.

I walked out of the room stealthily, mentally hearing Alec Harvey define the act of trespass. It looked as if only a halfhearted effort had been made to clear the house. A huge oak chest and a long roll of carpet still stood in the dusty hall. I was convinced that I was alone but a guiltily nervous feeling made me call out "Hello! Anyone there?" before walking up the stairs. There seemed to be an atmosphere of death and decay in the deserted house and I walked quickly along a gallery, opening doors on a succession of bare, dusty rooms. Each time I reached for a door handle I did it gingerly, as if dealing with something unpleasant.

A room right at the end of the gallery was smaller than the others, crammed in like an afterthought on the part of the builder. Oak panelling made it dark but it was free from the otherwise pervasive musty smell. The windows were also different, with smaller panes of glass that had a faint greenish tinge to them. On a panel halfway along one wall I found a carved Crusader's shield bearing the word "Paterini". There was no doubt in my mind that this room had served as a meeting-place for the English Paterini. I remembered the quotation I had found on Haswell's letter-heading which now appeared so appropriate: ". . . as a cult will survive centuries after its myths have been exposed and its sources of faith tainted. . . ."

Though the wind was still making a loud blustery noise against the ancient glass panes, I could also hear the sound of an engine. It sounded more like a car being driven quite fast in first gear than a plane, but I was anxious to see if Andrew was flying about trying to find a landing place. I could not open the green-tinted windows so I ran into the next room and pulled down a sash.

After searching the rain-laden sky I looked down to see that a red Range Rover was being driven round the house, having made a different approach to mine. I watched it stop by the front door with an unpleasant mixture of guilt and nervous tension. The driver's door opened and General Findlay-Duncan got out. He surveyed the house and our eyes met. He gave me the cold smile that he had directed at the backs of incompetent waiters at Nissaki. He was dressed in a brown plus-fours suit with a tweed cap. He leant negligently back against the Range Rover as he watched me, as if in no hurry to do whatever it was he had in mind. He had the knack of appearing intimidating while still and silent.

A door on the other side of the Range Rover opened and Mrs Marianne Prothero appeared. She too looked up in my direction and she called out in a throaty voice, "Oh yes, he's there! Look, Will! In Victor's room."

It seemed that the excitement of the chase had the same effect on Mrs Prothero as sexual arousal, and I immediately recognised the husky voice which had disturbed my slumbers at Theo's Taverna. In an instant I knew the identity of the couple who had crept into the unoccupied room above mine for their nocturnal meetings. I had a vision of Marianne Prothero crouching above the General, on heat with desire and excitement. Another vision too, of Mrs Findlay-Duncan sitting down to write the letter that had warned me of "the demented friends of the late Mr Townshend". I could see her extracting a stiff envelope from a cluttered drawer, then holding the letter in trembling fingers, trying to clear her fuddled brain, slowly reading over what she had written with worried, gooseberry-green eyes.

The General reached down into the Range Rover and

produced a walking stick and a bugle, lifting the bugle to his lips in a perfunctory way before bowing slightly in my direction. I thought yes, he's a cunning devil, he absorbed all that I told him, and perhaps a bit more, about my Korean experiences. He knows there is terror in the hearts of men and knows how to play on fear, but surely he realises I can deal with an ageing cripple and an overweight woman.

As if in answer to this thought the blond giant I had encountered in Carcassonne emerged from the back of the Range Rover. He rubbed his nose and nodded in my direction.

The General opened his blue eyes very wide and said, "I spy a trespasser, Carl. We must deal with him." He gave each word equal weight, as if reading from a prepared script. Carl said something in reply but I only caught the tones of his sing-song voice.

My feeling of guilt at having trespassed in the Townshend house had vanished. I was convinced that I was confronted by the trio who had contrived the deaths of Haswell and Reardon. I opened the window wider and called out, "Yes, I know who it is." I felt that I would back myself against the slow-moving giant who was a sucker for a left hook.

A moment later this feeling of confidence left me and I collapsed mentally like a bag of wind. If I was in a trap, then it must have been set for me by Jane Mackmurdo. This knowledge attacked me like a sudden fever. If Jane had lured me to Old Court, then she too must be one of the friends of the late Mr Townshend. I shivered, suddenly feeling cold and weak. And if Jane had lied, then Andrew Foster was not on his way to meet me. My brain feverishly formulated the wild theory that perhaps they had already dealt with him by sabotaging his plane.

I walked out of the bedroom and back along the gallery, unable to think straight. I climbed a dark, cramped flight of stairs like a robot.

On the next floor there were some poky servants' rooms

littered with crates and rubbish. Aimlessly I walked into a small room containing an antique pitted bath and a geyser. The dirty window began to register the first sideways dashes of rain, like unintelligible writing.

Again the sound of an engine drew me close to the cobwebbed window. I opened a stiff broken sash with difficulty and put my head out. This time it was a familiar sound, and a sight that delighted me. A small beige and cream aircraft was circling overhead. I could see the bold white letters GARFG clearly on its side. As I watched, the wings wiggled once and then the Cessna began a slow turn preparatory to landing on the parkland beyond a clump of oaks.

Fear fell away from me like the grossly exaggerated gloom of a nightmare. Jane had not lied to me and she had no part in the plot. Mr Townshend's friends must have had my telephone tapped and knew of my plan to visit their Cathar meeting place. I was in control of myself again. I walked downstairs, determined to deal with the friends of the late Mr Townshend.

27

"No RETREAT, no retreat. They must conquer or die who have no retreat." When I cautiously looked out from Old Court's massive front door it was obvious that General Findlay Duncan did not take that quotation too seriously; it was just a well-rehearsed piece that sounded impressive. When it came to action he preferred the pragmatic "discretion is the better part of valour". I saw that he was driving off at a fair turn of speed. The Range Rover sent up a shower of wet gravel as he made a sharp turn. Carl was hunched up in the back seat, having trouble in accommodating himself in what were to him cramped quarters. Marianne Prothero watched the descending Cessna, then stared solidly at me with her fleshy face pressed right up against the side window. Her expression was hard to describe, mingling malice and contempt with just a little puzzlement. Mentally she was shaking her fist at me.

The implied threat was a hollow one. My step was light and I whistled "Colonel Bogey" as I made my way through the rose garden that had become overgrown with convolvulus and thistles.

Rain fell steadily as I walked to greet Andrew. By the time I reached the Cessna my white windcheater had become a dirty beige colour. Andrew jumped down from the plane looking puzzled.

"The guests arrive and the guests depart. Who the hell was that?"

"Just some of Townshend's friends. General William Findlay-Duncan and Mrs Marianne Prothero."

"Good God! You're kidding!"

"Not at all. They were on very chummy terms, and they

had their heavy, the Swede, with them. The General threatened me, said I was trespassing and they would have to deal with me. If you hadn't arrived just then I might have ended up having an unfortunate accident. You see, I'm sure I've found out the answer to 'Do you know who it is?' Townshend's sister Viola. It turns out that she owns the elegant villa at Aghios Stephanos. My bet is that the Ormond Townshend family have acted as treasurers and defenders of the Cathar faith for centuries. But Dave and Ken must have believed they could find the Rennes treasure hidden in Miss Townshend's villa. So the 'friends' took up a defensive stance and the treasure-hunters...."

Andrew nodded silently for a few moments, reviewing all I had said.

"Hindsight I suppose old man, but now it seems to me that I was always puzzled about what the General was doing on that package trip. Never seemed to fit in or to be enjoying himself, if you know what I mean. Always sitting around looking bored stiff with his drunken missus, or mysteriously popping off solo in his Renault. I suppose it was on those trips that he reported to Miss Townshend, keeping her in the picture. Well, what do we do now?"

"Police. What else?"

"Yes, police. I happen to know an extremely bright detective chappy at Savile Row. Met him through a fraud case at the bank. He'll be able to tell us what we should do. But by God I bet it will be hard to prove anything. What do you think the chances are of any of Townshend's friends actually ending up in quod?"

"I know. Piss poor."